Omensford Series – Book 6

Fae & Familiars

G Clatworthy

ISBN: 978-1-915516-28-2

Foreword

The Omensford witches first arrived in my writing in <u>Attack on Avalon</u> (book 5 in the Rise of the Dragons series), but they were too interesting to leave there so they had to have their own book. And so, this series was born, based around the fictional town of Omensford in the Cotswolds and the witches who live there. Fae and Familiars sees Fi take a much needed break in Cornwall – one of my favourite parts of the UK – so this book is dedicated to my Cornish husband and his family, I hope I've done you proud.

A special thank you to my amazing typo hunters, grammar gurus, and plot pickers who got this story to where it is today. You are awesome!

If you want to support Gemma, you can find her on <u>www.patreon.com/G_Clatworthy</u> for exclusive first reads of new stories. You can also join her newsletter at <u>www.gemmaclatworthy.com</u> for a free short story based on one of the witches in the Omensford series and follow Gemma on <u>www.instagram.com/gemmaclatworthy</u>,

<u>www.facebook.com/gemmaclatworthy</u> or join the readers' group on Facebook: <u>Gemma's book wyrms.</u>

Chapter 1

Fi swerved and accelerated hard out of the corner, determined to win the race. She swung right, avoiding a box on the road then cursed as Mort overtook her. Fi accelerated again, willing the small car onwards as she took the short cut. With a smile, she sped up and made the jump dead centre, soaring over Mort's car with a gleeful smile.

She landed back on the road with a thud and kept going. Victory was in her sights. She dodged a banana left on the track and crossed the finish line with a fist pump.

"Yes!"

"Not fair, you used a shortcut!"

"Sorry, not sorry." She shrugged, unable to keep the smile from her face as her character celebrated on screen and did a victory lap.

"You bumped me off the track on that rainbow! I hope you drive better than that when you take your test."

Fi grimaced and checked the time on her phone. "Speaking of, I'd better go." She bent over and planted a kiss on Mort's lips. It was nice to be in a real relationship, not overanalysing every move or reading into every gesture. And if she wanted to kiss Mort, she could. But 'nice' was hardly a fitting word for the feeling of security, contentment and warmth she had deep inside her at this very moment – like a delicious secret or a perfect fudge cake – that meant she just knew that Mort was right for her.

If she were braver, she'd tell him how she felt, but that would mean discussing her feelings. And what if he realised he was too good for her? Even though her ex was long gone, the scars from that relationship still tugged any time she thought too deeply about her emotions. She would never be that vulnerable again. She settled for giving him another quick kiss. Actions spoke louder than words anyway.

He gave her a hug and whispered, "Good luck, you'll be great. And just think, this time tomorrow, we'll be in Cornwall."

Fi smiled, she was looking forward to their first holiday together; a whole week in a small flat overlooking the Cornish coast. But the driving test came first. She had finally decided to upgrade her provisional driving license to a full one, and she wasn't sure she'd made the right decision. Fi took to driving like her mother took to computers; as in pretending it wasn't something she needed to do, asking others to do it for her and only engaging when there was no other option.

"Are you alright with Cressida for a couple of hours?"

"I've already told you; yes! Now stop procrastinating, go!"

Aren't you going to ask me if I'm alright being alone with your lover for a couple of hours? Cressida, as always, spoke directly into her mind. Strange, for sure, but Fi was used to it. They had been paired for over a year and the bond had grown stronger over time.

Fi pulled a face at her familiar's question. The small golden wyrm knew that she hated the term 'lovers', it sounded like something out of one of the romance novels her sister read rather than real life.

"I know you'll be OK; it's Mort I'm worried about."

Mort chuckled and patted Cressida on the head. The dragon-like creature scoffed and lowered her head back onto her forelegs, curled up in a sunny spot by the window.

Get out of here, I can feel your anxiety and it's making me queasy.

Fi pulled a face at her familiar. Since they had both embraced the familiar bond between witch and wyrm earlier in the year, both of them now experienced each other's feelings more viscerally. And Fi wasn't surprised the wyrm felt her nerves; the butterflies in Fi's stomach were more like the flying goombas she fought in videogames. Cressida would be absolutely fine. Still, Fi dithered.

"Go!" Mort shooed her out of the door. "I'll meet you at your mother's after the test."

She sighed and pulled her hood up as if that could help protect her from the anxiety spiralling in her stomach. Fi hadn't even been able to face a cup of coffee, or a bacon sandwich this morning, a sure sign her nerves were out of control. The last time she had been this nervous, she had shorted out the entire school just before an exam. No, she wouldn't think about that. Her electrical power was under control now, not like when she had been a teenager.

She marched to her sister's house. Agatha had offered to drive her to the test centre and let her use her car for the test. Fi had agreed, but now further doubt settled in her mind. The 'car' was a massive pick-up truck, and she had only driven it a couple of times. She should have hired a smaller car for the test.

Fi ignored the small voice inside her that said her nerves weren't only about the test. This was her first proper holiday with a man since a disastrous break with her ex, where she'd spent the entire time trying to find a decent wifi signal and coffee, ignoring the many couples' activities he'd planned. Camping under the stars might sound romantic, but there hadn't been a working toilet, let alone a shower. And then he'd insisted on toasting bread over the campfire because it was 'what you do when you go camping'. It took over fifteen minutes to get two charred pieces of toast without anything to go on it because they hadn't thought to bring any and the nearest shop was a half hour walk away. Fi wasn't the nicest person on an empty stomach, so, several choice words later, they had left that same morning. Two days early.

And Fi couldn't shake the spiralling feeling that Mort might want more of her than she could give. It was a reflex left over from her relationship with the clingy Li, and it washed over her in dark waves the moment she thought she was happy.

What if Mort had only booked a cottage to try to make her happy, but he hated holidaying inside?

What if he wanted to camp on the cliffs and watch the sun rise?

Fi paused at the low hung gate that led to her sister's house. Her treacherous feet had led her here while her mind wandered. It wasn't too late to back out. Why did she need to drive anyway? She could always catch a bus…or continue to cadge lifts off her sister. And, if that failed, she could fly on the vacuum cleaner she used in place of a broom.

Too late. Agatha strolled out of the front door and shooed away the chickens that clustered at her feet. "How did you lot get out of the back garden?" The large rooster – Cluck Norris – pecked at her crocs. "Go on, get. Morning Fi, ready for the big test?"

Fi swallowed and nodded. She couldn't back out now.

"Come on, you always want to be independent. What could be more self-sufficient than driving your own car? Besides, it's a lovely, sunny day so you won't have to deal with poor visibility or slippy puddles."

She hadn't even considered driving conditions. The goombas became Pac Man ghosts chasing her down. Fi followed her sister to the car. The enormous pick-up loomed over her. What had she done? How could Agatha be so optimistic that Fi could control this beast? This was a mistake.

"I don't know Aggy…"

"Come on, you've practiced. I know you can do this."

It was hard to argue with her sister's unshakeable optimism, so she took the easy path and got in the car, grateful that Agatha was driving to the test centre.

Chapter 2

It took forty minutes to drive to the nearest test centre in Swindon, although it felt like the time raced away. Every time Agatha overtook a bumbling lorry on the narrow country lanes, Fi was glad she would be taking the test in a town.

All too soon, they arrived in a bleak industrial estate and Agatha reverse parked into a spot that didn't seem wide enough to take the car. Fi groaned. Reverse parking wasn't on the test syllabus, but parallel parking was. What if she had to try to guide the monster truck between two other cars? Under her skin, her magic flared and she forced it back down. Now was not the time to lose control and fry her sister's car.

"Let's get you checked in, then." Agatha paused, then reached a hand over and placed it on Fi's shoulder. "You'll be fine. You got this."

Fi nodded weakly and traipsed after Agatha to the test centre; a grim, grey building that might as well have a sign over it saying 'abandon hope all ye who enter here'. She headed inside.

The efficient but unsmiling staff handed her a clipboard and told her to complete the paperwork before they could sign her in. She had to fill in forms agreeing to the test, confirming her details and handing over her provisional license for scanning. Agatha produced insurance documents and signed some sort of waiver. Then they waited. Time slowed to a treacle pace.

Fi tapped her foot on the polished concrete floor, her nervous energy needing an outlet. Agatha frowned at her.

"Will you stop that?"

But Fi couldn't stop. She had to move. She pushed herself up from the plastic chair and paced the waiting room, noticing that she was the oldest person taking her test. The others were fresh faced teenagers staring at their smartphones and posting about their upcoming exams.

"Why is it taking so long?"

"Uh, Ms Blair?"

Fi whirled around.

"I'm Dave. I'll be your examiner for today. If you'll follow me, we'll get started."

"Yes, right, of course." Fi wiped her sweaty hands on her trousers and held out her hand. He took it, shook it once then gestured to the door.

"This way, Ms Blair."

"Fiona, please call me Fiona."

"Good luck Fi," Agatha called with an accompanying thumbs up.

Fi swallowed and followed Dave out of the door. He pointed to a neon orange Volkswagen Golf parked across the road. It had a spoiler jutting out from its hatchback roof and gold alloys on the wheels. Classy. "Can you read me that number plate?"

Fi nodded and read out the letters and numbers printed on the yellow plastic. "U R 4 N O B. Hah. You're a nob."

The examiner pursed his lips and made a note.

"No, I wasn't calling you a nob – it's the number plate…"

"And, I believe this is the car that you'll be driving today." He walked up to the huge pick-up and stopped by the bonnet. Fi hung her head and followed him over to the car. *What kind of person chose to have that phrase on their car's official license plate?* There must be easier ways to insult people than with a novelty number plate.

"If you can pop the hood and tell me how you'd check for oil," Dave said.

The tech witch fumbled with the keys as she unlocked the car and searched for the button to unlock the bonnet. She found it and heard the click as the hood popped open. Scrambling back to the front of the car, Fi opened the bonnet fully and pointed to the yellow dipstick handle, glad that Agatha had drilled her in this.

"Show me."

Fi fiddled with the dipstick and pulled it out to show him that it was at the right level. He nodded. "OK, let's get in the car." He climbed into the passenger seat and strapped himself in, holding his clipboard up, ready to make notes.

Fi swallowed and chided herself. She'd practiced. She was always better at practicals rather than written exams and she'd passed the theory test first time. Of course, that had been on a computer, which was a lot more familiar than handling a two-tonne vehicle. She closed the bonnet and got into the car, tripping slightly as she stepped up so she fell in rather than climbing in gracefully. Fi gave the examiner a small smile and strapped herself in.

"When you're ready, start the engine."

She pressed the ignition and the car roared to life. Fi offered up a silent communication to the car as she gripped the steering wheel. *Please don't mess up, or break down, and please let me find the bite point smoothly.*

"When you're ready, tell me how you'd check the brakes are working."

Fi recited the textbook answer she'd found on the internet about making sure brakes aren't spongy and checking as you drive off. Dave nodded and ticked a box on his list. Fi breathed out, maybe this wouldn't be so bad.

"And when you're ready, drive out of the carpark and turn right."

Fi adjusted her mirrors – she'd heard it was one of the things they tested for – put the car into first gear and pulled out of the space with only the slightest of jolting motions as she found the bite point of the clutch.

Chapter 3

Fi's shoulders relaxed as the examiner gave her instructions to turn right, then left, then left again. She remembered to indicate at each turning and check both ways before coaxing the car to the right direction, and the three-point-turn she had executed in the side street had been a sweet bit of manoeuvring, even if she did say so herself.

The only slight wobble had come when she had waited for ages for a gap in the traffic to pull out of a junction. As the cars passed, her hands became pricklier, and her anxiety spiked. *Did they mark you down for not being assertive enough in traffic?* Eventually there had been a break in the cars and she had pulled out. She peeked over at Dave. He made a mark on his clipboard but said nothing. She swallowed. It would be fine.

And then she saw it. The most terrifying sign in Swindon; the magic roundabout. Fi breathed out a curse word then glanced at the examiner; he didn't seem to have heard her.

Just her luck to get a driving test route that took her over that hellmouth.

It was made of five mini roundabouts, arranged in a pentagon, and rumours in the magical community suggested it was a seal. Although no one could agree on what exactly it sealed. Some people thought a demon was captured underneath, others that it lay over a portal to another realm, filled with monsters. Why else would the town planners have agreed to such a bizarre road configuration?

Either way, everyone agreed it was a pain to drive over. Fi used a different expression in the privacy of her own head as she slowed and joined the queue of cars approaching the demon roundabout.

"Sorry, could you repeat that?" Lost in the horror of the traffic abomination, she hadn't heard the instructions on where to go.

"At the roundabout, turn right."

"Right. OK. Got it." Fi's palms sweated on the steering wheel and her magic swirled to the surface at her anxiety as she picked a lane. The crazy configuration meant that she could go right at the first roundabout, then right again at the second and pull off, but she was already in the wrong lane. She decided it was worse to pull across three lanes of traffic, so she stayed in her lane, meaning she had four roundabouts to cross instead of two. Maybe that would give her extra marks. The examiner pursed his lips but kept quiet.

All too soon, they were at the front of the queue and Fi eyed the oncoming cars for a gap. There. She accelerated forward and made it over the first roundabout, and, with a streak of luck, straight onto the second. She calmed her breathing and forced her magic down as she signalled and waited to get onto the third roundabout. A white van driver let her out in an uncharacteristic show of charity, and she shot him a wave as she crossed the roundabout before lamping her hand back on the steering wheel. Always keep two hands on the wheel, unless indicating or changing gears. Three down, one to go. And that was where it went wrong.

Too nervy, Fi pressed the accelerator instead of the brake and shot forward to a chorus of angry beeps from other cars. She carried on, staring straight ahead, unable to face Dave in the seat next to her. Out of the corner of her eye, she noticed he gripped the seat instead of the clipboard. That wasn't good.

He didn't say anything about her blooper, and carried on directing her in his monotone voice, until they got back to the test centre, where she misjudged the size of the truck and mounted a kerb. She braked abruptly.

"I've failed, haven't I?"

"If you can park the car, Ms Blair, I'll give you your results."

Fi swallowed and found the biggest parking space she could, swinging the car into it at an angle. She swore. Dave's face was three shades paler than when they'd set off. He took a couple of minutes to total up his tallies.

"I'm afraid you haven't passed, Ms Blair. I've noted two majors and seven minor faults. Here's a copy for you." He handed her a sheet of paper from his clipboard and opened the door with a shaking hand. "Enjoy the rest of your day."

Fi stared at the flimsy piece of paper, evidence of her failure to drive, and looked at the black crosses in the fault boxes. They faded to blobs as tears blurred her vision. She sniffed and rubbed her eyes, annoyed that she would cry over something as stupid as a silly driving test.

"How'd it g–?" Agatha asked chirpily at the window, before she noticed Fi's tears. "Sorry, love, but never mind, hey. You can try again another time."

Fi nodded. "Guess you're driving back." She got out and walked stiffly to the passenger seat.

Agatha drove off in silence as Fi texted Mort to tell him they were on the way back. He replied asking how her test went. She'd left that out of her first text.

I failed.

A few seconds passed, then:

Sorry about that, the examiner was probably too intimidated by your driving prowess.

Fi snorted out a laugh, then went back to staring out of the window to avoid Agatha's curious glances.

They were halfway back before Agatha broke the silence.

"Come on, it's not like it's a car-tastrophe."

Fi's lips twitched, her love of puns overtaking her self-pity. "I car-n't believe you are trying to make a joke of this."

"I thought it was pretty engine-ious."

"Brake it off, Aggy."

"I car-n't."

"I used that one already."

"Alright, you win. But you know, it's really not the end of the world. It took me three goes to pass my driving test, and it's not like there's a time limit."

"I know, I just… I thought I was ready, you know."

"And this way, Mort will have to do all the driving in Cornwall."

That didn't make her feel any better.

"How about I treat you to an ice cream."

"I'm not a child, Aggy!"

"I know…but everyone likes ice cream."

Chapter 4

Fi stuffed the last of the wafer cone into her mouth as Agatha pulled up outside their mother's house, a three-storey Bed & Breakfast that Fi had moved back into after losing her job, and hadn't moved back out of.

"I'll come in with you."

Fi shook her head. "No, I'd better tell her myself."

"I want to say hi to Mum, she'll want company while you're gone."

Fi thought that her mother was looking forward to having some time to herself, but Agatha was better at reading other people's feelings.

Fi got out of the car and squared her shoulders before heading round the back with her sister; only guests and strangers knocked on the front door of the Bed & Breakfast.

Her mother sat at the kitchen table, a pot of tea in front of her as her fingers moved a crochet hook in complicated patterns, forming wool into an item of clothing for her granddaughter.

"Hi Mum."

"Fi, how did it go?"

She took a deep breath. "I failed."

"Sorry to hear that." Nell offered her a small smile. Better than beration for failing, but her mother's sympathy still grated. "Still, you can try again."

Fi nodded. Her mother was nothing if not practical.

"Agatha, lovely to see you."

Agatha grabbed a mug from the cupboard and settled down at the table, helping herself to the remains of the pot of tea.

"You're staying then?" Nell asked between stitches.

"I thought I'd pop in and say hi before I pick Bea up from her friends."

Nell nodded and bent her head to her crochet.

"Well, I'm just going to grab my suitcase then I'll be off," Fi said.

"Enjoy your holiday."

"Do you need anything before I go?"

Her mother put down her crochet. "Fiona, I have run this Bed & Breakfast since before you were born, and I lived alone for years when you moved out. I think I can manage for a week; we've only got two rooms booked."

Her mother was annoyed with her for going on holiday then.

"I'm not annoyed that you're getting a break."

Fi stared at her mother. Nell claimed her powers didn't extend to mind reading, but sometimes Fi wasn't so sure.

"Go on, your doctor will be waiting for you."

"You're sure you don't need anything?"

"Just bring me back some fudge. Now go!" Her mother made a shooing motion with her hands then huffed as a stray piece of wool got caught.

Agatha mouthed "Told you" over their mother's head and sipped her tea.

Fi hurried upstairs and grabbed her suitcase. She considered taking another console, but she'd already packed her laptop and two portable gaming consoles, and they were going on holiday to spend time together, not play videogames. Not for the first time, she wondered if this trip was a good idea. Apart from the disastrous camping holiday with her ex, she hadn't been on a vacation in over a decade, preferring to spend her holidays playing marathon gaming sessions. But, she hadn't been with someone she'd wanted to spend time with before. With a final look at the PS5, she headed out of the room.

She patted the doorjamb as she left her bedroom. "Take care of Mum while I'm gone," she whispered to the house. Fi didn't know exactly how the magic worked, but the semi-sentient house shuddered as if it agreed to watch over the older witch. Fi patted the door again and headed downstairs, bumping the suitcase on every step. The house flicked the carpet under her feet in retaliation at the bumps and Fi stumbled. With a muttered apology, she carried the case down the remaining stairs and into the kitchen, where Mort waited with her mother.

"I didn't hear you come in." Her words sounded accusatory, so she shot him a smile to take the sting out of them. "I mean, I wasn't expecting you."

"I thought I'd wait in here rather than in the car."

"He's been keeping us company, and he appreciates a good cup of tea," her mum said.

Fi rolled her eyes. She preferred coffee, was that so bad? Apparently yes in her mother's book.

"Why don't I take your bag to the car so you can say goodbye?"

Fi mouthed "Coward" at Mort as he took the black case out to the car.

"Well, bye then," Fi said.

"Have a great time." Agatha stood and pulled her into a hug.

Fi brushed her mother's cheek with her lips.

"I'll be fine, go!"

Fi left, following Mort out to the car. She climbed in and he handed her a box.

"What's this?"

"I got it to celebrate your test."

"But I failed."

Why don't you just stomp on his heart? Honestly, Fiona, he's doing something nice for you. Cressida raised her head up from her spot in the back seat. Fi opened her mouth, but Mort replied before she could say anything.

"Then it's a good job I'm not going out with you because of your driving skills." He planted a kiss on her lips. "Open it."

Fi eyed him. Mort had a grin on his face. He expected her to love whatever was in the box. She opened it with shaking fingers; she had bad experiences with gifts. Just because she was female, her ex assumed she wanted flowers and chocolates, and her sister seemed determined to buy her the ugliest presents imaginable. Fi still had her eyes set on a hideous gnome to return the gesture, but she hadn't found one that was bad enough. She shook herself out of her daydream and tore open the rest of the wrapping, ready to pretend to love it.

Her eyes widened and she pulled out the plastic case. The latest karting game from Nintendo. A grin spread across her face. She already had the game, but it was the thought that counted. He knew her.

"I thought you could brush up on your driving." Mort sounded nervous. "But if you don't like it, I can take it back. It was thoughtless, sorry."

Fi reached up and pulled him towards her for a long kiss. "It's perfect. I love it."

He grinned like a schoolboy. The house banged its shutters loudly as if to say they should get a move on. Fi rolled her eyes. "We'd better get going. Sorry I can't help with the driving."

"Nonsense, I wouldn't have asked you to tackle the M5 on the same day you passed your test anyway." Mort pulled out of the crescent shaped driveway and headed south towards

Cornwall. Fi smiled. She might not have passed her test, but she was about to have a romantic getaway with the man she loved. At least, she thought it was love. Her mind skittered away from the intense emotion. Maybe it was a hard like. She was happy though. She was sure about that.

Chapter 5

The car journey took six long hours through traffic and Mort had been happy to sit in silence listening to an audiobook for the most part while Fi scrolled on her phone, occasionally sharing titbits of interesting facts about Cornwall – who knew it had once been considered part of the fae realm? – and snapping pictures of her familiar sleeping for her online gaming friends. But Fi could see the signs of stress in his tight jaw and the way he insisted on only one pee break. It wasn't until they finally pulled up to the small sea front cottage they had rented for the week that the tension melted away.

A large blue bug hit the windshield with a splat. They both jumped. Fi stared. The bug was a humanoid shape with blue skin and large glittering, black eyes. Its transparent wings shuddered as it tried to take off again.

"Use the wipers."

Mort stared at her in horror. "I can't do that, look at it, poor little thing. I've got to go and help it."

Fi privately thought it would be kinder to put it out of its misery, but she followed Mort out of the car.

"What is it?"

"Piskie, izza?"

They both jumped at the growling voice behind them. Fi turned to see a bent old man, holding a stick. She had never seen a weathered face before, but this man had lived through the elements. Every wrinkle spoke of days outside on the sea, no matter the weather.

He reached out and grabbed the creature before stuffing it into his pocket. Fi and Mort stared.

"Pain in the arrrrrse, wanee. Bloody faeries. Joan the Wad stirring up trouble, eenshe?" he mumbled with a strong Cornish accent. "Ye rrr frrr the room, izza?"

"Pardon?" Mort asked at the same time as Fi said "What?"

"The room," the man enunciated with a roll of his eyes that declared exactly what he thought of tourists.

"Oh, yes. Seaview Cottage."

"Aye. That'll be it. Keys." He shoved a keyring at Mort. "Jus' up thar. Tharr's milk in fridge. Diddy need nawt else?"

"Er, that's lovely, thanks," Mort answered. Fi saw the tension back in his jaw. He had no idea what the old man had said either.

"Nee problem. Faathurgotun iffee need enthing. Welcome to Kernow, bleddy emmets." The old man rolled off with a gait that should have been on the deck of a ship instead of walking down the paved driveway. Fi had to stop herself swaying from side to side as she watched him veer off into another, larger house at the end of the drive.

"I think we just met our landlord for the week."

"Did you understand anything he said?" asked Fi.

"Nope, but we've got the keys. Let's explore."

Fi smiled at Mort's enthusiasm and followed him into the house.

"Erg." Fi shook her foot. "Why is there a bowl of milk on the doorstep?"

Maybe they have a cat? Cressida peered around, searching for the animal.

Fi rested her hand against the rough stone wall and undid her converse trainer. Now it was going to smell like stale milk for the entire holiday. Brilliant.

The cottage was quaint, made of grey slate stone that seemed to sink into the cliff behind it. Someone had painted the windows a cheery eggshell blue that contrasted well with the dark stone in the fading daylight. It was exactly like the picture Mort had shown her online.

With a cry of triumph, Mort found the right key and opened the door. "After you." He bowed her through, and she laughed, never sure how to take his chivalry.

She dumped her suitcase just inside the door and flipped a light switch. The interior was painted entirely white, including the wooden floor. Fi slipped off her converse trainers, not wanting to smear mud or milk on the pristine floor. Mort followed inside, bringing the other case.

"What's that?" Mort nodded towards a wicker basket in the centre of the faux marble kitchen table and Fi stepped over to explore.

"Looks like a welcome basket…pasties, Cornish tea, scones and a note – 'clotted cream in fridge with milk'."

"That's nice."

"Do you think that old pirate did this?"

"Doesn't seem in keeping with his idiom." Fi raised her brows at Mort, and he elaborated. "Style."

Fi nodded and finished rooting around in the basket. "They could have included coffee."

"Check the cupboards."

Fi opened the off-white wooden cupboards and found tea, a tin of tomatoes, a pack of porridge oats, some cooking oil and, right at the back, a small supply of coffee. "Ugh, it's supermarket brand."

"We'll get you some coffee tomorrow, you caffeine snob."

"I just know what I like."

"Really? And what would you like right now?"

Fi swallowed at the promise in his voice as he moved closer, but her stomach grumbled loud enough that he could hear. As if in conversation with each other, Mort's stomach joined in. She patted his jumper.

"I think we should eat first. I'll get the pasties."

A tentative knock sounded on the door just as she took a bite out of the meaty half-moon shaped pasty. Fi answered it, her mouth full of buttery pasty pastry.

"Hi there, sorry I wasn't here to welcome you. I had to take the dog to the vets." A sad looking collie sat at the woman's feet, looking up at Fi with big, brown eyes. The woman stuck out her hand. "I'm Tamsyn. You found us alright?"

"Er, yes." Fi thought that was pretty obvious, after all, they were in the cottage.

"Good, good. And the journey down?"

"Bit of traffic."

"OK, well you're here now. Honestly, it's nice to get someone in the cottage, what with all the pest problems on the news, people have thought twice about booking. Anyway, did Da tell you everything you needed to know?"

"Er, he gave us some keys and kidnapped a pixie."

"Piskie." Fi's puzzled look caused the woman to give an explanation. "Not a pixie, a piskie. They're unique to Cornwall, some sort of fairy, I think. Sorry about that, he's an acquired taste." The woman screwed up her face and fiddled with the long, beaded necklace strung around her throat. "I can see you found the pasties, anyway. They're from the local bakery."

"Oh, you're behind the basket. Thank you."

"Yes, of course. And, er, you said you had a pet? We love animals, but…I've never seen a wyrm up close before…"

Fi recognised the hint in the woman's voice. "Cressida, come here, would you?"

Why?

"You've got an adoring fan."

Naturally. The wyrm came to the doorstep and preened as the woman oohed and aahed over her golden scales. Fi relaxed as Cressida allowed the woman to stroke her, only hissing when the dog got too curious and tried to sniff her tail.

"She won't burn the place down, will she?"

"No, she's house trained."

Cressida's tongue flicked out in annoyance, but she didn't say anything.

"And you've paid the pet bond, so that's all good."

Pet bond? What about a Fiona bond? You cause more mess than I do.

"Do you have a cat?"

"Hmm? No. Why?"

Fi looked down at the plastic bowl she had dunked her foot in upon arrival. The woman tutted and scooped it up. "Sorry about that. Da likes to put something out for the piskies, says it brings him luck. Well, if you need anything, I'm at the lodge just there. Enjoy your stay." The woman called her dog to heel and walked back to the house at the end of the drive.

"Who was that?" Mort appeared behind Fi and wrapped his arms around her.

"The lady behind the welcome basket. Apparently, Wurzel Gummage was her dad."

He laughed, then pulled her back inside.

"What are you doing?"

"It's our first night away on holiday and I'm looking forward to having you all to myself."

Fi smiled and allowed him to pull her to the bedroom.

Chapter 6

"This is nice." Fi surprised herself by voicing the thought out loud. She swung her legs against the stone wall. It was pleasant. The breeze played around her hair, making her glad she had a light jacket on over her top. The low sun was an orangey red ball as it hovered on the horizon, turning the calm sea into a glowing fire. The perfect end to an idyllic day of walking across the beach, paddling in the surf, and a bit of shopping in the local supermarket. The patchy internet down here had barely tarnished her mood, which was, perhaps, the most surprising thing of all.

"I'm glad you like it, I wasn't sure you would."

"Really?"

"Well, it's outdoors, the signal's not great…"

"I like other things than technology."

Mort gave her a look and took a chip from the bag they were sharing.

"I do!" Fi popped a crunchy chip in her own mouth as she thought.

Yes, you love living in a tip.

Fi frowned at the small wyrm and gave her a chip. Her room was often a mess, but that wasn't her defining trait, surely. "I like baking."

And eating. And sleeping...

Fi snorted. "Are you sure that's not you?"

Cressida gave her a look and took another chip.

"Are you sure she's meant to have those?"

"Probably not. No more chips for you, Cressida." The golden wyrm eyed the thin slice of potato in Fi's hand. "I mean it." Fi held it higher, out of her reach.

With a blur of blue, a piskie dived at them and grabbed the chip out of Fi's fingers. She cried out and let go and the creature sped off, chattering in triumph.

"Hey!"

Fi's mouth hung open as the small piskie wobbled in flight, carrying the chip that was nearly as long as it was. It landed on the sand and started to devour it with pointed teeth when a seagull approached.

The piskie gnashed its teeth and held the chip behind its back as it shook a tiny fist at the large gull. While it was distracted, another piskie darted up and grabbed the fried potato. The two piskies fought, yanking the chip until it fell to the sand. The original piskie pushed the newcomer, who launched itself at the first piskie and they disappeared in a flurry of sand, rolling over and over, shrieking as they fought.

The seagull took the opportunity to peck at the discarded chip and fly off triumphantly.

"Bloody piskies," a man walking his dog said as he passed.

"Are they always like that?"

"Most times, they stay out of the way up on the moors, but this year," he shook his head, "they're everywhere. I've never seen anything like it. Worse than the seagulls. You best keep your chips close if'n you don't want 'em stolen."

With a tip of his cap, the dog walker went on his way. Fi took another chip and stuffed it in her mouth, glancing side to side for incoming chip stealers, so focused on the brawling piskies on the sand that she didn't notice the gang of piskies that popped up from behind the wall.

"Hey!" She swatted at one as they each grabbed a corner of the chip bag and beat their wings furiously, trying to lift off with it. Mort swiped at one on the other side, but it dodged and clawed his hand.

"Ouch!"

Cressida snapped at one as it buzzed by her head, and flicked her tail in annoyance, sending the bag of chips tumbling to the floor. The piskies swarmed the fallen food and chomped noisily on the fried potatoes.

"And here I was thinking Cornwall was tranquil," Mort said with a shake of his head.

"First world problems."

"I suppose."

"And you're wrong."

"Oh?" Mort's brow crinkled with confusion.

"About me only liking technology."

"Really?" He raised an eyebrow.

Fi pulled him towards her and gave him a lingering kiss. "I like…" She chickened out. She couldn't admit her feelings out loud. It felt too committal. "…kissing you," Fi finished. Lame. What was wrong with her? Why couldn't she articulate her feelings? Was it so hard to admit she liked Mort, maybe even loved him? Her mind baulked at that, uncomfortable even thinking about loving someone after her experience with Li. He had wanted to hear it from her all the time and now the word stuck in her throat. Just when she thought she was done with him, her toxic relationship with her ex reared up to destroy her present.

Really? Kissing him? Cressida's disappointment rang in Fi's head.

Mort simply smiled. "That sounds like something I can work with."

Fi's phone rang, interrupting their intimate moment. Fi pulled it out of her jeans pocket to turn it off when she caught sight of the name flashing on the screen. Why was her boss calling?

Chapter 7

It was Agent Jones.

"Hello?"

"Fi." Agent Jones was as brusque on the phone as she was in person. "I've had reports of a piskie problem in Cornwall. And there's been a murder. I know you're on holiday, but I'm short staffed and you're there anyway…"

Fi sighed.

"I'll owe you."

The thought of Agent Jones owing her a favour was intriguing.

"OK, what do you want me to do?"

"As far as we can tell from the reports, the piskies are acting unnaturally bold and attacking tourists."

"Yeah, they stole my chips!"

"Right…they killed a tourist yesterday." That put the chip theft in perspective. "Maxi's got a theory. I'll hand you over."

The shifter shouted for the other agent and then Maxi's voice came over the phone.

"Fifi! On hols, yah? Cornwall's absolutely spiffing this time of year, I remember one time we went to the old holiday home and got so bladdered that–"

"Get on with it, Maxi." Fi heard Agent Jones shout from the other end of the phone.

"Yah, well, there are fairy stones, or fae stones, if you want to be accurate." A sharp cough sounded from his superior and he carried on. "Anyway, they can cause magical creatures to act aggressively. I think that's what's happening. Well, either that or they've got a strain of rabies which presents as similar symptoms, but let's hope it's not that, what? Or one nasty nip and tourists will go mad."

Fi blinked at the phone. "Can I speak to Agent Jones?"

"Yes?"

"So, you want me to try to find some magic stones to stop these animals, but it's possible it's rabies."

"The likelihood of it being a disease is practically zero. Have you ever heard of an infectious disease that only targets tourist spots? Anyway, see if you can get to the bottom of it before they pass a law to class the creatures as pests."

"I thought they were already classed as pests."

"Everywhere outside Cornwall. South of the Tamar, they're protected, but they won't be for long if they keep attacking people. The dzraking fae representative is nowhere to be found. I've got Whitehall breathing down my neck here. And don't get me started on the Royal Society for the Protection of Magical Creatures."

"That's a lot of people breathing on you."

"Just sort it."

The shifter hung up.

Fi rubbed her eyes and stared out at the evening sky, now painted in ominous orange pastels by the setting sun. This was meant to be a relaxing holiday with her boyfriend.

"Sounds like they need you." Mort couldn't disguise the hurt in his voice.

"Sorry, I'll make it up to you."

He raised an eyebrow. "I might take you up on that."

She smiled, slow and sensuous.

"Besides, I rather like the idea of being a detective," he said.

"Huh?" His sudden change in conversation topic had her head spinning.

"Well, you'll need some back up on whatever this mission is, right? And I'm here. We can work together, it'll be fun." He jumped off the wall and looked back at her. "Come on."

"You want to start the investigation now?" Her seductive smile clearly needed work. He nodded and yanked her off her perch.

Back at the cottage, with a mug of hot chocolate in hand, Mort ran through what Fi had told him.

"So, the Magical Liaison Office thinks that someone is making the piskies act aggressively using magic rocks?"

"Yep."

"And they're about to pass a law in parliament declaring them as pests and ridding the piskies of magical protection."

"Yep."

"And we've got to find out what's going on and stop it."

"Yep. And don't get bitten; in case it's piskie rabies."

"OK. Where do we start?"

"Er, we do some research."

"Of course. And that means…"

"We look up the latest incidents online, then go check them out tomorrow."

"Not tonight?"

"It's easier to see in the daytime."

"Right, so you're saying we've got the night to ourselves…"

Fi curled up closer on the squashy sofa. "That's exactly what I'm saying."

Cressida stomped out of the room. *I'm going to bed if you two are going to start canoodling.*

Chapter 8

The next morning, they walked to the nearest café in search of a wifi signal. Fi inhaled the fresh sea air as they strolled past quaint little houses and shops, dodging cars as they skipped across the road.

Well, Mort skipped. She stumbled. He hadn't shut up about the case and what might be causing it. She hadn't even had time to taste her morning coffee, made with the most expensive instant brew the local supermarket had to offer, when he dragged her out of the door, declaring that fresh air was a better wakeup call than coffee. Did the man not know her at all? He then glared at every loose stone as if that might be the cause of the piskies' strange behaviour.

Fi thought it was almost poetic that one of them flew straight into his face then shook its tiny fist at them before it flew off in wonky zig zags. Even Cressida gave a snort that may have been a laugh. The two of them shared a look as Mort stared after the fae creature.

She needed that coffee. Fi dragged Mort into the café that proclaimed 'free wifi' on its sign and sucked in a deep breath, allowing the bitter scent of coffee mixed with baking bread to lift her spirits. She ordered for herself and drummed her fingers as Mort chose something more exotic than his usual cappuccino because he 'was on holiday'.

Fi kept up the tapping on the counter as the young barista went through the motions of making the drink. *Come on, how long does it take to tamp down beans?* On a whim, she ordered a slice of chocolate cake to go with her coffee, after all, she was on holiday too, and two rashers of bacon for her familiar. She regretted her impulse as the server stopped what he was doing and plated up the slice of cake before walking the bacon order to the kitchen.

"Make that two cakes," Mort called from the corner where he had found a table. Fi suppressed a sigh as the young man took his time selecting the second slice and plating it up.

What's taking so long? Cressida called from her spot on a chair next to Mort. *Did you remember my sparkling mineral water?*

Fi wished the psychic connection went both ways because there was no way she could insult the server out loud.

He paused as he handed the plate to Fi. "Are you eating in?"

Fi gave him a look. "Yes," she ground out and her foot tapped in time with her fingers.

The server nodded and went back to the drinks. Five long minutes later – Fi counted on the huge clock that took up half of one wall – he finally placed the drinks on the tray, and Fi took everything over to the table. She placed the tray carefully, not spilling a drop of the precious elixir as she unloaded the drinks and the cakes, before she got her laptop out of its bag and set it up.

Mort opened his mouth to speak but Fi held up one hand to silence him as she took a sip of her coffee. She breathed out a sigh of pleasure. Much better than sea air.

"Now, I'm ready to talk."

He smiled at her. "I think I like you in the morning. Very assertive."

"Trust me, you don't. Did you find anything?" she asked as he handed her the card with the wifi password.

"Piskies are a type of fae – am I pronouncing that right? – they're a protected species in Cornwall but outside of the county they're counted as pests. They have distinctive blue skin and are shy, retiring creatures that prefer to stay in the country, although in modern times, some have moved to the city and scavenge the food available there. They don't much like the sea, something about the salt in the water…Locals often blame them for minor mishaps…Then there's a load of theories about where they came from and how they ended up here…their queen settled here…or they were banished from the fae realm…this bit says that Cornwall actually belongs to them…"

"OK, where did you get that from?" Fi opened up the Magical Liaison Office application on her laptop to add in some details. She saw that Agent Jones had already assigned her a report to complete.

"Er, Wikipedia."

Fi gave him a look. "That trusted site." She patted his hand to take the sting out of her words. "But it's a start, I guess." She pasted the web address into the background section of the report, wincing as she never liked to rely on crowd-source edited websites for facts. "Let's see if there's anything in the MLO database. Can you find any recent piskie disturbances?"

Mort turned back to his phone as Fi bent over her laptop. The MLO database didn't have much on Cornish piskies and Fi frowned as she recognised some of the text that Mort had read out; it looked like the Office didn't have her qualms about using editable websites for their sources.

"There was an attack at Tintagel Castle two days ago..." Mort gasped and showed her his phone screen. "Someone died!"

That matched up with what Agent Jones had told her. Fi tapped frantically on her keyboard as Mort continued.

"And a couple was treated for minor abrasions after visiting the popular site when a swarm of piskies attacked and drove them off."

Fi found the same article on her computer and read on. The couple had been coming to Cornwall for years…this was the first time they'd experienced anything like this…ruined their holiday…will be spending the rest of their time at the beach. Blah, blah, blah. Then there was a quote from a Demelza Zennor, an expert in piskies; 'They're usually shy and retiring creatures who avoid people. I don't know why they're acting up this year, perhaps it's due to the extreme weather conditions. I mean we had that mini heatwave last month. And we are the ones who invaded their territory, we can tell from ancient remains that they lived here before we settled in Cornwall. Maybe it's time they stood up for themselves.'

Fi snorted. Two guesses who had been behind the Wikipedia entry.

Mort looked up from his phone. "So, what's the plan?"

"Let's go sightseeing."

Chapter 9

Fi stared out of the car window as Mort pulled into Tintagel Castle's car park. The sun glared down from a sky scudded with tiny clouds. They reminded Fi of her familiar's scales, or maybe the skin of a larger, more dangerous monster.

"Not many people here," she noted.

"Maybe they heard about the attack. Those piskies are vicious."

Fi nodded. They got out of the car and headed to the ticket office. Cressida paused by a metal bowl of water outside the office and gave Fi a meaningful look. She sighed and asked for two tickets and a bottle of sparkling mineral water for her familiar, who supped it from the lid with satisfied slurping noises.

"That's thoughtful to have water for dogs. Why have you got milk as well though?"

"Oh, that's for the fair folk," said the English Heritage volunteer as he took payment for the tickets, his wrinkled hand shaking as he handed them over.

"What?"

Pardon. Cressida could never help correcting Fi.

"The fair folk. Lords and ladies."

"They're names for the fae," Mort said.

"Right, yes. Of course. Why do you leave them milk?"

"It's just what you do. My grandmother did it, my mother did it, now I does it. Keeps them happy."

"Does it work?"

He shuddered. "It didn't work when them piskies attacked the other day."

"What happened?"

"Well, it was all over so fast. I don't know zactly how it started but I hears a scream and the piskies swarmed over the tourists. I thought we'd have to close, but head office said the risk assessment was fine. I put up signs though." He pointed a gnarled finger at a handmade sign of a blue fairy with WARNING spelled out in large black letters. "Try not to disturb them. And carry some iron on you."

"Iron?"

"Fae folk don't like iron. Here, we sell these in the gift shop." He placed two iron brooches in the shape of Celtic crosses on the counter. "That'll be ten pounds."

Fi raised her eyebrow, but Mort paid and fastened the brooch on her top, planting a kiss on her forehead when he was done. "Lovely."

Fi couldn't help smiling as she shook her head at the superstition and the upselling volunteer, who's eyes sparkled as he watched them, no doubt wondering what else he could get them to buy from the gift shop. She pinned the second brooch onto Mort's t-shirt and they headed over the modern bridge connecting the mainland with the rocky outcrop where the castle perched. A cloud crossed over the sun and Fi shivered, wrapping her arms around herself. As she gazed down at the white-capped waves lashing against the rocks below, she thought she caught sight of someone looking back at her. She gave a cry of surprise, but then the face was gone.

What's the matter?

"Are you alright?" Mort asked.

"I thought I saw someone in the water."

Mort peered over the wire railings at the cerulean sea, there was nothing there. "Probably a seal."

Honestly, you scared me half to death. Cressida's tone was sharp, but she nuzzled against Fi's legs, seeking comfort. Fi bent down and scratched her golden head.

"Maybe." Fi looked away from the sea and up at the remains of the castle. "It's a bit…creepy, don't you think?"

Mort looked at her as if she was mad. "It's just some ruins, and no signs of piskies yet. Come on." He took her hand in his and pulled her forward. She hoped his enthusiasm would wear off soon. Maybe this was the reason that detectives liked to work alone in crime films. At her feet, Cressida followed so close to her ankles that Fi tripped over her.

They wandered through the imposing grey ruins and Mort stopped to read every single sign about the place. Fi kept her eyes open for any enchanted objects that might cause piskies to attack visitors. Cressida stayed by her feet, flicking her forked tongue as she scented the air.

"Is this it?" Mort asked, holding up a pebble.

"Stop bringing me pieces of rock! Do you really think we're just going to stumble over a magic stone in the middle of the castle?" Fi dropped the stone back on the ground. She had pocketed the first two striped stones Mort had given her as a fun memento of their trip, but this was ridiculous.

"Just trying to help."

"I know, sorry. It's just…this place. It's getting to me, like it's pressing down on me." Fi shuddered. Her power swirled under her skin, always more active when she got anxious.

I can feel it too. It's as if something doesn't want us here.

"Cressida feels it too."

"Maybe that means we're on the right track."

"Maybe…"

"Come on, I want a photo of you by that giant statue of King Arthur."

I don't like this place.

"We'll go soon, come on, let's get this picture."

The eerie feeling weighed on Fi more and more as they got closer to the oversized bronze statue of the ancient king. Even with the sun on it, it looked like some sort of wraith out of middle earth.

"You want a picture of me with that?"

Mort nodded, beaming as he held up his phone. "Maybe we should get a selfie."

He draped an arm around her shoulders and grinned up into the screen. Fi plastered on a smile, doing her best to ignore the persistent cloying sticky pressure around her. Mort snapped the picture and brought it up on his phone to show Fi.

"Wait. What was that?"

Fi peered at the flash of blue on the screen.

Chapter 10

She whirled round, drawing her power to her palms in a crackle of electricity. At her feet, Cressida hissed. A piskie zipped across the sky and landed on Arthur's crown. It cocked its head and regarded them with huge bug-like eyes.

It bared spiked teeth and let out a high-pitched chittering sound that echoed around the cliffs.

"Maybe I can talk to it, do you think they understand English?"

Mort shrugged.

Fi stepped forward and lowered her hands. She raised her voice, locking eyes with the piskie perched on the aged statue. "We are here to help you," she said slowly in the time old tradition of English people speaking to foreigners. "You have to stop attacking people."

It tilted its head to the other side and blinked its glittering, black eyes.

"I think I got through to it–" Fi's words turned into a cry as the piskie launched itself at her, pushing off of Arthur's head and flying straight for her face, gnashing its pointed teeth.

She threw her hands up in a defensive pose, power flowing into her palms. The piskie collided with her electrical magic with a sharp pop and fell to the ground.

"At least it's only one–" Mort choked off partway through and pointed.

More of the creatures climbed over the cliff edge, pouring over the rock in a tide of blue skin and translucent wings, eyes trained on the witch standing by the statue. Fi took a step back, pulling Mort with her. Hundreds, maybe a thousand of the palm-sized critters swarmed over the cliff, turning the ground into a strange blue sea as they moved forwards.

"I think we should go…"

Mort nudged her side and jerked his head backwards. More piskies crowded behind them. Fi swallowed.

"What do they want?"

Mort's jaw tightened and he squeezed Fi's hand. There was a long pause as the piskies surrounded them, their clacking chittering filling the air. On some unspoken cue, a hum reverberated over the rock. Fi looked around, then realised that it was the sound of thousands of tiny wings beating. The piskies launched themselves upward, blocking out the sun with their blue bodies as they closed the trio in.

I think they want to kill us. Cressida shrank down to the ground, her belly close to the rock and eyed the critters.

"Did you hear me? You have to stop hurting people."

"I don't think they can understand you." Mort backed up against Fi.

One of the piskies screamed and pointed its tiny index finger at the trio. The piskies took up the cry and dived forward.

Fi coated herself with her fizzing magic and spun, ducking in a vain attempt to avoid the massing fae creatures. They sparked off her magical shield like they hit a bug zapper and dropped to the ground in a daze.

Mort had his hands up, protecting his head from biting piskies. Fi took a step towards him, maybe she could make her shield larger and protect them both. Her mouth dropped open as a sword appeared in his right hand. His posture changed and he took up a fighting stance. The piskies sank back, baring their teeth at the new weapon. Since she had learned to sense magic, Mort's sword gave off a glorious rush of energy, an otherworldly power mixed with sharp stabs of pain if she concentrated on it for too long. Her strong magic meant she only felt it when she tried to sense it, but she didn't blame the piskies for giving Mort and his sword a wide berth and focused on Fi and the wyrm.

Cressida holed up under the statue of King Arthur, snapping and hissing at piskies, her wings stretched out from her back, scything round as the creatures crowded her. She snapped her jaws as one got within reach, tearing the piskie from the sky and biting it in two before breathing a jet of fire out in a wide arc from her hiding place.

In here, she spoke in Fi's mind.

Fi sprinted over, directly through the buzzing piskies, who fell to the floor with a pop. Fi grimaced as the stench of burned flesh filled her nostrils. She crouched next to the statue and peered in, trusting her magic to protect her against the onslaught of fae creatures. Cressida flicked her tongue at a small, smooth stone with a perfect circle cut through it.

"What is it?"

Can you sense it?

Fi closed her eyes. There was a strange pressure pushing on her, but nothing specific. "I need to drop my magic," she huffed in frustration. Her power was so strong that it clouded her senses to other magic, but through the familiar bond with Cressida, she was able to siphon some of her magic away for a short time. That was no use here, though. If she dropped her magic, the piskies would swarm her.

"Mort, can you keep the piskies away while I check this out?" Fi shouted.

Mort nodded and strode over, cutting a swathe of the blue creatures down as he went. They weaved away from his sword, shaking their fists and dive bombing his head before whirling away to avoid the blade of death that could cut through anything.

He planted himself in front of Fi and circled the blade, creating a wide arc that kept the piskies at bay.

Fi concentrated and dimmed her magic, flowing it into the familiar bond she shared with the golden wyrm. Cressida's emerald eyes sparked with electric power. She hissed in triumph and her body lit up with blue-white light. A piskie mis-timed its dive and collided with her scales, fizzing to the ground with a crack.

"I didn't know you could use my power!"

Concentrate on the stone.

"Right." Fi turned back to the circular pebble and held her hand over it, pushing her magic down so she could pick up any traces of another power. A piskie tangled in her frizzy hair, making 'ack-ack-ack' sounds close to her ear. She batted it away and Cressida leapt, teeth bared as she chased the small creature away from the witch.

Fi took a breath and tried again. A strange sickly sensation washed over her and sank into her back teeth. "Ugh, it's like I've eaten too many sugary foods," she moved her jaw, trying to get rid of the sweet taste that coated her tongue.

Fae magic.

"This must be what's driving them crazy. OK, I'm going to pick it up."

"Are you mad?" Mort yelled over the deafening hum of tiny wings beating and insectoid creatures chattering.

"Maybe."

Fi snatched back some of her power and coated her hand before she palmed the stone. The chittering changed pitch to angry screams. This was definitely what the piskies were trying to protect. She held it aloft and they all swarmed around her, diving at her hand. Fi gripped it tightly and blasted it with more of her power, but nothing happened. The stone stayed as it was, still emanating its candy floss magic, driving the piskies into a frenzy.

Fi yelped as one of the creatures raked its claws over her skin. The iron brooch was no deterrent for its frenzied attack. She yanked her power back from Cressida and coated herself with electricity once more. The piskies whirled around in a hurricane of swirling blue fae, dive bombing her fist.

Through the shimmering bodies, she glimpsed the sea. Piskies didn't like the sea. Mort had said that, hadn't he? She rummaged through her pocket and grasped the rough pebble there.

"You want a stone, have this!" Fi flung the stone up and inland as far as she could. The piskies swarmed to it with a high-pitched shriek.

Why did you give it to them?

Fi ignored her familiar and sprinted in the opposite direction. She threw the fae stone off the cliff and watched as it tumbled towards the sparkling sea. The piskies' chattering turned to angry screams as they realised her deception.

Fi swore. She'd thought that would work. She spun round, electricity sparking off her hands, ready to face the swarm. The creatures gave her a wide arc as they streamed past, the air from thousands of tiny wings buffeting her skin as they dived off the cliff after the stone.

"No!"

The circular pebble tumbled in slow motion, turning over and over as the piskies raced towards it in a blue-black cloud. Just before it reached the ocean, a pale hand reached up from the lapping waves and snatched the stone from the air. Fi blinked and it was gone.

The piskies hung over the water for a long second. Their angry buzzing became muted as the trance caused by the stone lifted and they flew away from the water with a sudden spurt of susurrated panic at being so close to the sea. Nearer the cliff head, many of them turned their heads this way and that as if searching for a reason why they were away from the ground. One of them flew into another, who swatted it back with an annoyed chirp and the piskies flew away along the coastline to wherever they made their home in a lazy, confused swarm.

Chapter 11

Fat drops of rain pelted the car as they drove back to the holiday cottage. The houses that had seemed quaint this morning now squatted in the foreboding landscape, shuttering their secrets as if the whole of Cornwall was telling tourists to get out and leave them alone. Fi hadn't quite believed Agent Jones when she'd said someone was controlling the piskies, but now…

Her phone rang, interrupting her train of thought.

"Aggy?"

"Hi Fi, I thought you should know that Mum's had a fall–"

"What?"

"No biggie but she fell and broke her leg yesterday–"

"What?!"

"She's back home now–"

Fi pulled at a strand of her frizzy hair that had worked its way free from her messy bun. "Do you need me to come back?"

"No need to worry, we've moved back home to help out. Bea's enjoying the change of scenery and Neville can work from anywhere really since his firm got that new meeting software–"

"Aggy…"

"So I'm dealing with the customers when I'm not at school–"

"Aggy! You're a teacher and you both have full time jobs."

"It's fine, really, and you'll be back in a few days, then you can take over. You know me, happy to help. And Bea's really cheering Mum up."

"Is that your sister?" Fi heard her mum's voice call. "Put me on." There was a short, muffled exchange as Agatha handed over the phone.

"I'd love a cup of tea…" her mother said, followed by a long pause and the sound of a door opening and closing as Agatha left the room. "Fiona, you have to get back here."

"Mum? What are you talking about?"

"Your sister, she's driving me mad."

"Come on, Mum. It's only been a day."

"Exactly."

Fi chewed her lip. She'd assumed because her mother and sister were similar, both in personality and magic type that they got along better with each other than with her.

"It can't be that bad…"

She imagined what it would be like to be stuck at home with Agatha fussing around after her, and shuddered.

"It is."

Fi thought for a moment. If she left Cornwall, who would deal with the piskies? "I'd love to Mum–"

"Excellent, I'll let Agatha know. When do you think you'll be back?"

"Mum! Listen. I'd love to, but, I've got a job to do here and I don't know when it'll be done. You'll have to live with Agatha for a week. It won't be that bad, you've got so much in common." Like how you both like to interfere with other people's lives. "And it's not like she didn't live with you before she moved out."

"How could I forget the teenage years?" If her mother was back to sarcasm, then she must be feeling better.

"Aggy's not a teenager, Mum."

"Fiona Blair, I am your mother–"

"Here you are, Mum, a nice cup of tea. You drink up while I say bye to Fi."

Another rustle as the phone passed back to her sister.

"So, as you can see, we're doing quite well here."

"Yep, Mum said." Fi kept the irony from her voice.

"OK, I'll call you if anything else happens, but really, just enjoy your holiday. Got to go, Mum's just spilled some tea on her crochet. Byeee."

"Bye."

Fi stared at the phone. Her mother never spilled anything. This broken leg must be affecting her, or perhaps Agatha's ministrations were causing her stress. She frowned at the phone, torn between the desire to help her mother and the need to do her job. Strange. That had never been a hard decision before; her job had always come first. Maybe she'd gone soft since she'd caught feelings.

"Something wrong?" Mort asked as he pulled into the drive.

"Mum, she's broken her leg."

"That's awful. Do you want to go back?"

"I can't, I've got a job to do here. And she's fine. Agatha's looking after her."

"How did it happen?"

"A fall," Fi scrunched up her face. That didn't sound like her mum.

"You sure you want to stay."

A vision of herself waiting on her mother hand and foot while her leg healed played through Fi's mind. "Absolutely."

Chapter 12

Back in the cottage, Mort sank onto the plush sofa and placed two mugs of coffee carefully on the low pine table. Cressida scratched her ear with her back foot and curled up between them, radiating heat.

Miraculously, none of them had been seriously injured in the piskie attack, but Mort had insisted on treating the minor scratches on Fi's hands with antiseptic and plasters that he produced from a travelling medical kit in the boot of the car. One of the perks of travelling with a doctor.

"So, we know that it's fairy stones not rabies. That's good, right?" He peered over the top of the large white coffee mug, studying Fi's face.

"Yeah."

"You don't sound convinced."

"Well, we still don't know who's enchanting the rocks and why, or where they are."

Mort tapped the side of his mug with his fingers. "So, what do we do now?"

Fi stared at the rain splattering against the window. She sighed. "I guess I'd better write up that report. Not much point looking for piskies in this weather."

"OK, what can I do?"

"Er, see if you can find out anything about the attacks."

He shot her a puzzled look, his dark eyebrows drawing together.

"You're a doctor, right?"

"And?"

"So, call up the hospital and see if you can find anything out about those people who were attacked. They'll tell you."

"That's not how the medical profession works."

"Can you try?"

He met her gaze and Fi felt like she was in some sort of staring contest, before he broke away. "Fine, I'll call the hospital, but don't expect them to tell me anything."

"Great."

He stood and took his phone into the bedroom to make the call. Fi pulled her laptop towards her and flipped it open, glad she'd brought it along. She opened up the report and added details about the attack at the castle and the fairy stones. She drummed her fingers on the arm of the sofa as she stared at the 'Next Steps' section. What were they going to do next?

"Can you stop scratching? I can't think."

Now you know how I feel about your incessant typing.

"My typing is helping us solve a case."

Yes, but do you need to be so violent? It's as if you're fighting the keyboard.

"I type with purpose. Ugh." Fi brushed a dull scale off her arm and onto the floor. "Keep your shedding to yourself."

Fi looked up the local coroners' office and fired off an email asking for details of the dead tourist and cause of death, but she suspected it wouldn't add anything except images for her imagination to worry over at night.

Her phone bleeped and Fi checked her messages. "Wow, Cressida, ten thousand likes for a picture of you."

What picture?

Fi cringed. "One I took of you asleep in the car."

I beg your pardon.

"I didn't know they were going to share it. I only sent it to some friends."

Cressida gave her a look.

Mort walked back into the lounge area. "I called the hospital."

We will talk about this later, hissed Cressida.

Fi winced, knowing she was in the wrong and, worse, Cressida knew it and would hold it over her. She focused on the case. "And?"

"They can't disclose patient details over the phone."

Fi let out a snort of annoyance.

"But, I left a message for the patients to expect a visit from the Magical Liaison Office."

"Brilliant."

"Visiting hours are between six and eight p.m. and it'll take us a while to drive up to Truro, so I thought maybe we could grab some dinner there."

"You're a genius."

"I know. I'll book something…as soon as I get some signal. The wifi's out again."

Fi typed in 'interview witnesses' to the next steps and got their details from the news article Mort had found earlier in the morning while he roamed the room trying to book a table for later.

After a few minutes, he pocketed his phone and moved in front of Fi. "So, what's my reward?"

Fi closed the laptop with a snap. "I can't think of anything right now…"

"Really?"

"Maybe if we moved to the bedroom, I might get some ideas…"

Oh, just go already and leave me in peace. At least then I'll know you can't take pictures of me while I'm sleeping.

Chapter 13

Mort swung his large four by four into a tight parking spot outside the Royal Cornwall Hospital and paid the parking fee while Fi walked inside. The building's sloping roof was clad in slate tile and someone had decided that it was a good idea to paint the window surrounds in red to contrast with the white front of the building. It reminded Fi of blood. Not a good omen.

Mort joined her inside and they walked to the reception desk together.

"I'm looking for Mr and Mrs Gabberwaith."

"Mrs Gabberwaith was discharged earlier today, and Mr Gabberwaith has been moved to the Minor Injuries unit."

Fi followed the signs to the ward, hugging herself as she walked down sterile corridors with off green floors. "Why do hospitals always smell weird?"

"It's the cleaning fluid, they've got to be as sterile as possible so there's less chance of infections spreading, and you don't want to know the sorts of things the porters and cleaners have to clear up."

Fi stopped dead in her tracks. Mort was right. She did not want to know. With a shake of her head, she scurried after Mort who hadn't broken his stride while he imparted that tidbit, she knew he was a doctor, but it wasn't natural being so at home in a hospital.

He stopped at a door and sanitised his hands before buzzing to be let into the Minor Injuries Unit. He held the door as Fi sanitised her own hands and walked through.

"Mr Gabberwaith?" she asked a nurse in a tight uniform that stretched over his torso so much, he looked like he might hulk out of it.

"Bed three."

Fi walked past the bright blue curtains that surrounded each bed. They were probably meant to look cheery, but instead heightened the institutional feel of the ward.

A short man sat propped up in bed with a thick bandage wrapped around his head and another around his arm. A woman sat on the chair next to him, leaning forward and pecking at a cereal bar with quick, darting movements.

"Mr Gabberwaith?"

"Yes? You don't look like a nurse."

"No, my name's Fiona Blair, I'm with the Magical Liaison Office and this is Dr De'ath. I wanted to ask you some questions about the attack. They should have told you to expect us."

His grey eyebrows shot up at Mort's name, but he kept quiet and studied Fi's I.D.

"Oh, it was awful," his wife said, flapping her arms and sending crumbs flying onto the floor. "We were minding our own business, just viewing the castle, as you do – we're on holiday you know, it's our twenty-fifth anniversary and we had our first holiday away together on the coast –"

Mr Gabberwaith captured one of his wife's hands in his own. "They don't want to know our entire backstory, dear."

Mort picked up the chart on the end of the bed as Mrs Gabberwaith took a breath.

"Yes, well, as I said…" She shot her husband a look. "…we were minding our own business when I noticed them. I said 'Look, there's piskies,' – we've been to Cornwall practically every year, only missed it when we decided to try somewhere new, but Spain's just too hot so we stick with Cornwall – anyway, we haven't seen them up close before, they're usually a flash of blue then gone, so I took some pictures because these weren't scared of us at all, were they Roy?"

Fi blinked as Mrs Gabberwaith continued without taking a breath.

"Then, before I know it, they attacked me. Roy did his best to fight them off, didn't you, love? But there were so many, and the little blighters kept on at us, didn't they, love? So we ran for it. We were in the car before I noticed the blood and then Roy called an ambulance, didn't you, love? And they were very good, I must say, but we were kept in overnight to monitor for rabies, and poor Roy has had an extra night due to the head injury."

Fi looked at Mort for confirmation as Mrs Gabberwaith wittered on, and he nodded. The chart matched their story.

"But they think he'll be out tomorrow, don't they, love? Mind you, I don't think we'll stay on for the rest of the holiday, one of the nurses said the piskies have attacked so many tourists he's lost count."

"And did you notice anything strange at all?"

"Nothing. One minute it was fine, next we were surrounded by the beggars, weren't we, Roy? I yelled to run, didn't I, Roy?"

"You said we needed to get the dzrak out of there."

"Roy! I never swear."

"OK, thank you, I get the picture. Did you see this man?" Fi held up her phone with a picture of the deceased on it.

"Yes, he was wandering around too, taking pictures up by the King Arthur statue. Poor thing, he was covered with the creatures. By the time the ambulance got there, it was too late. I couldn't look."

"Covered in blood, he was." Roy stared at a spot over Fi's shoulder, his eyes glazed as he remembered.

"Thank you, you've both been very helpful." She left them to the rest of their visiting time and led the way back through the warren of corridors.

"Well, that was a waste of time. They're just some random tourists.

"Not a total waste, we can still have our meal."

Chapter 14

Fi stayed silent, brooding as Mort drove away from the fake cheerful hospital to a car park in Truro. She allowed him to lead her through the grimy underpass and into the city.

"Do you want to go home?"

"Huh?"

"You haven't said a word, and you're clearly not in the mood for a meal. Let's go home."

"No." She took his hand. "I want to go out. It's just this case, it's ruining our holiday."

"It's not ruining my holiday. It's sexy to see you in action."

She gave him a playful shove with her shoulder and snorted. Sexy? As if. She was a mess. And detective work was dull. And they'd been attacked. No, sexy was not the word she'd choose. They turned into an open square by the cathedral with its towering spire, the cream stone underlit so it appeared to be something from another world, almost magical. Fi shook her head, she should be enjoying herself, not stewing about oversized bugs. "Let's get some dinner."

He opened the door and gestured for Fi to walk into the Italian restaurant. She did and almost collided with a mirror set up to make the tiny place look twice the size. A waiter shook her hand, his shirt cuffs unable to fully conceal his swarthy arms, and led them to a small table in the corner. He produced a long lighter with a flourish and lit the tall, red candle stuffed into an empty chianti bottle on their table, before handing them menus and bowing away.

"Sorry, I didn't realise this place was such a cliché from the website."

Fi placed her hand over his. "I love it. I feel like we're in Lady and the Tramp."

"We should get spaghetti."

Fi felt her cheeks heat at the suggestion in Mort's voice. She leaned forward and kissed him on the lips. "You don't need pasta to get a kiss."

The smell of burning curled into her nostrils, more pungent than the aroma of garlic bread that wafted around the restaurant. She swore and waved the menu that had caught the candle flame. The small fire burned brighter. Mort grabbed the menu off her and threw it to the ground, where he stomped on it with his fancy brown loafers.

He picked it up and placed it on the table. "Looks like we'll have to share." He passed her his menu, giving the candle a wide berth and Fi stared unseeing at the words as her entire body went red with embarrassment.

What had she been thinking? Her impulsive and romantic gesture had almost set the restaurant alight. She wasn't cut out for this type of thing. The server came back as all Fi's misgivings about the holiday crowded around in her head. She stared up at him and mumbled an order of pizza and diet coke.

He gave her a pained look. "I am sorry bella signora, we do not serve pizza here."

What sort of Italian restaurant didn't serve pizza? "Er, take his order first." Fi blinked to clear the tears that had crept into her eyes and read the menu. Flowery Italian names in a hard to read font dared her to choose them. She searched desperately for something she recognised, gave up and chose a random pasta dish.

Mort gave her an odd look as she ordered, then leaned forward as the waiter left. "I didn't know you liked squid."

"Is that what calamari is?"

"You didn't know?"

Fi swore.

"We can swap when the food gets here."

"You don't mind sharing?"

"Not with you."

"What did I do to deserve you?" Fi clamped her mouth shut as soon as the words were out.

"I could ask myself the same thing."

"No, really. Why be with this," she gestured to herself, "when you could have anyone?" There. She'd said it. She'd voiced the queasy unease that sat in the pit of her stomach. "I mess up the simplest little things, I can't even have a proper holiday…"

"Stop." The command in his voice drew her eyes up to meet his. "I am having a great time. I enjoy being with you, not someone else. And don't refer to yourself as 'this', it's demeaning and negative self-talk."

"Sorry."

"I didn't say it so you would apologise, I think you should be kinder to yourself. I wish you could see yourself through my eyes."

"Oh?"

"You'd see a smart, sexy woman with a great sense of humour and a body to die for, even if she does hide it under slouchy clothes."

"I knew you hated that jumper."

"I don't hate it, it means you save all those curves for me."

"You're not half bad, you know," Fi said.

"I know."

"And so modest."

"It's not exactly modest when your girlfriend calls you 'not half bad'."

"How about amazing, kind, caring, fantastic…"

"Keep going."

"Handsome, brilliant, wonderful…"

"I'll drink to that." Mort raised his glass and Fi chinked hers against it, smiling.

"So, what do you think we should do next?"

Fi sighed. She'd almost succeeded in forgetting about the bloody piskies. "I think we've seen everything there is to see on the Tintagel attack. So, I guess the next step is to talk to that piskie expert."

"Right." Mort pushed his glass around on the chequered tablecloth.

"What's wrong?"

"There's a lot of talking to people and waiting around, isn't there?"

"What were you expecting? A high-speed car chase?"

"Not exactly…"

Fi laughed, and the tension in her body left as the giggle bubbled out of her mouth. It was just too funny. They were meant to be on holiday, and Mort was annoyed that they weren't working more. Mort's mouth quirked upwards and then he laughed too. It was all so ridiculous.

"Let's not talk about piskies anymore tonight. Tell me something about yourself. Something embarrassing," Fi said, steering the conversation away from work.

An endearing twinkle came into Mort's chocolate brown eyes and he took a sip of red wine. "Well, there was this time when I was just starting in practice and a patient came in with asthma. I had to listen to her breathing so I put my stethoscope on her chest and say 'big breaths'. Her eyes open so wide, I think she's about to pass out, then she takes a step back, puts her hands on her hips and says 'Excuse me?'

"And I have no idea what I've done, but I'm terrified because she's a heavy-set lady and I'm a stick thin graduate in my first practice placement, so I say 'I want you to take big breaths' and she gets a glint in her eye and laughs right in my face. 'I thought you were hitting on me when you said big breasts.'

"I turn the same shade as this tablecloth and I don't know where to look, but I get through the exam, and ever since I ask patients to take 'deep breaths'. What about you?"

Fi wiped a tear of laughter from her eye and took a drink, catching Mort's gaze. "There was this one time I pretended to have heart problems so I could see a doctor about some medicine…"

Mort's smile widened. "That was when I knew you were special, when I saw this gorgeous witch walk into my practice and lie about heart problems. I almost told you to come back in a week just so I could see you again."

Fi snorted. "You never."

He nodded. "So, that's not an embarrassing story."

"OK, did I ever tell you about the time I ruined the school disco?"

He shook his head and leaned back in his chair.

"This will be hard to believe, but I wasn't very popular in secondary school." Mort made a scoffing noise in the back of his throat, but Fi held up her hand to stop the interruption. "It's true. But I was good with electronics, and Agatha was part of the school committee organising the dance, so she asked me to do the lighting.

"It started off great. I worked with the kid who was DJ-ing and programmed in sequences to go with all the different music. Everyone enjoyed it, bopping along, doing the macarena – all the cool stuff –and I got to sit with the lighting system instead of dancing awkwardly on my own – I wasn't exactly popular, and no one asked me to go with them.

"But then I got cocky. I decided to improvise to Cotton Eye Joe and override the programme with a new combination. I made those school lights work harder than they ever had, but I got too excited, and I couldn't control my power as well as I can now…" Fi let a small thread of electrical power trickle over her fingers like a sparking piece of spaghetti before extinguishing it.

"…and the shock shorted out every light in the school. Everyone had to go home. I didn't tell anyone it was me, of course, but people knew I was unlucky with electrics…I'd already blown up the computer lab, and Agatha knew…"

"I'm so sorry."

Fi shrugged. "It's in the past."

"I meant, I'm so sorry none of the idiots danced with you."

She shrugged again. It didn't matter. That's what she told herself as the sting of rejection and loneliness from her schooldays rolled over in her chest. Mort reached for her hand and pressed it to his lips, the warmth of his mouth grounding her in the moment.

"Would you dance with me?"

"Now?!" Fi stared around the restaurant.

"Why not?"

She could think of a million reasons: there was no space between the tightly packed tables, the fire hazard of the candles, the ambiance music wasn't exactly made for dancing, people would stare… But she was spared from speaking by the arrival of the food.

"Let's eat."

"OK, but I still want that dance."

Fi nodded and took a bite of her calamari pasta. It had a pleasant tang of lemon and some sort of herbs that worked well with the rubbery squid. Not bad, she thought as she took a second bite. Not as good as pizza, though.

Back at the cottage, Mort pulled Fi into his arms, twirled her around under the starry sky, and kissed her. Maybe dancing wasn't so bad.

A low chuckle made her turn. The old man sat on a bench. He waved. Something small moved in his other hand. Was that the piskie?

Mort spun her round and she giggled. So what if the old man stared. They were allowed to be young and happy. Fi allowed Mort to lead her backwards until her back pressed against the door, trapping her between his warm body and the cold hardness of the wood. She fumbled with the keys while returning his kiss and then they tumbled through the door into the soft light of the cottage. Fi couldn't think. She sank into the moment, enjoying the warmth of his lips against hers and the length of his muscular body pushing against her as he swayed them to the beat of some imaginary song.

Her feet hit something hard, and she fell to the floor with a curse, pulling Mort with her.

"What's that doing there?" She glared at the coffee table.

Mort stood and pulled Fi upright, then they both gazed around the room.

Furniture lay at strange angles in the moonlight, making the chic holiday let look like a jumbled mess. Had there been a burglary? Were they closer to solving the mystery than she thought, and someone wanted to warn them off? That sort of thing happened in films, but not so much in real life.

A glint caught Fi's eye and she bent and pulled a golden scale from the corner of the low coffee table. She rubbed it between her thumb and forefinger and looked up.

The TV cabinet wobbled. She sprinted across the room, hurdling over the sofa to get there as the TV screen juddered closer and closer to the edge. Fi caught it just in time to save the deposit.

"Cressida! What on earth are you doing?"

It itchesssssss.

Chapter 15

The next morning, the house looked tidier, but the small wyrm looked worse, despite several hot oat baths – a sure fire treatment for shedding according to the internet.

"Yes, thank you, I understand." Fi hung up the phone, glared at the handset and threw it onto the sofa.

"No luck?"

She shook her head. "That's the fifth vet and none of them will see her. They say she's a special magical case. What are we going to do?"

So itchy.

"Stop that!" Fi jumped up and pushed her familiar away from the coffee table. Mort crouched down and gathered up the moulted scales. "You're just making it worse." She softened her voice and scratched down the dragon-like creature's back. Cressida shivered with pleasure.

"We can't leave her here."

"No, she'll destroy the place."

'She' is right here.

"Well, you will. You'll have to come with us. And I'll keep ringing around the vets."

Fi bundled her familiar into the car and Mort headed for the small town where Demelza Zennor had her shop. He glanced over his shoulder at the wyrm rubbing herself all over the leather seats, shedding scales on the plush upholstery, almost as much as he looked forwards during the drive. Fi bit her lip, feeling guilty on behalf of her shameless familiar. Mort's jaw ticked.

After she apologised for the tenth time, Mort had enough. "I said it was alright. She can't help it."

"I know, but…your car."

"It's fine. It's just a car."

Fi decided not to press it further. He was a caring and understanding person – more so than she deserved – but even he had a limit, and she was impressed it hadn't already been surpassed by the shedding wyrm now dragging her butt over the seat like a strange lizard dog, her forked tongue lolling out from between pointed teeth.

"This is it. It says her shop is halfway up the High Street… There!"

Mort swerved at Fi's shout and waved an apology to the car on the other side of the road. Fi sank down in the seat and kept her eyes trained on the shop fronts. Yesterday's rain clouds had thinned into the same scale-shaped tufts as yesterday and the sun flicked through, providing rippling patches of light along the street. A crystal twisted in one of the shop windows, refracting the light into a pool of rainbows. That had to be the shop.

Mort parallel parked the car with an ease that reminded Fi of her failed test. He was so darn perfect, it was almost annoying. Almost. Or was she trying to find something wrong with him? What was wrong with her? This amazing man was on holiday with her and hadn't shouted at her when her familiar had moulted all over the car, and, instead of appreciating that, she focused on the pangs of jealousy eating away at her stomach because he could manoeuvre a car. She shook her head, telling herself to get it together, gathered Cressida from the back seat and headed towards Demelza's shop.

She swatted aside the beaded curtains that hung across the entrance and stepped into a dark shop. Incense crowded her nostrils. Cressida squirmed her way free and jumped onto the floor, her claws clacking on the black and white tiles.

"Hello? Miss Zennor?"

"Yes?" A pile of clothes spoke from a corner.

Fi moved closer. "Miss Zennor?"

"I am she, proprietor of Zennor's Emporium of Magic, how may I help you?" The pile of clothes stood, and Fi saw that it was in fact a squat woman wrapped in a deep, purple cloak. "Are you looking for something in particular?"

A soft, scraping noise caused both of them to turn. Demelza eyed the wyrm as she dragged her slender body along the corner of a display of tarot cards, leaving a trail of golden scales in her wake.

"Sorry, she's shedding." Fi picked her up.

"It's not shedding; it's scale rot."

Impossible. I am a clean wyrm, I cannot possibly have rot.

"Are you sure?"

Demelza raised one bushy eyebrow. "Of course, I'm sure. She's losing her glossy gold scales and the ones underneath are a burnished brassy colour."

She was right. Cressida was slowly turning a dull colour, as if her gold was tainted. The small wyrm covered her face with her front paws.

"How did she get it?"

"Could be anything. But the sea air won't help. Wyrms need it hot and dry, any wet weather can aggravate scale rot."

"Oh Cress, I'm so sorry."

Fi knew her familiar was upset because she didn't even bother to correct the witch when she shortened her name.

"Don't worry. It's perfectly curable. Here," Demelza dug around in a stack of creams. "Try this." She handed a small pot to Fi.

She read the label. "Dragon polish. What's in it?"

"Herbs, beeswax, all anti-fungal. It will stop the rot and the itching."

Fi opened it and sniffed the cream. She pulled her face back from the pungent ointment, screwing her nose up at the medicinal tang. "What do you think, Cressida? I still can't find a vet who'll see you, this could be our best bet."

Cressida shrank back from the pot, her nostrils quivering. *Just get it over with. I'll try anything to stop this itching.*

Fi dipped her fingers into the cold, slimy cream and rubbed it over her familiar's body. Cressida shuddered under her touch, rubbing against Fi's hand, helping to spread the ointment over her scales.

So cool.

Fi grimaced. Her fingers started to tingle, but she continued lathering the cream over Cressida until the wyrm was covered from head to clawed toes in the white substance.

"You'll have to apply it twice a day for a week, but it should stop the rot."

Much better.

"Thank you."

"Not at all. And you should probably give her one of these twice a week to prevent another outbreak." Demelza placed a pack of tablets on the counter. "That'll be fifty pounds."

Fi paled.

Don't look like that. I'm worth it.

As Fi handed over her card, her fingers brushed Demelza's and the taste of coal filled her mouth. Weird. She stuck her tongue out. What did coal even taste like? The sensation left as quickly as it began, and Fi dismissed it as the effect of the cloying incense that hung around the shop.

Demelza handed Fi a receipt. "But I don't think you came here for wyrm ointment or pills."

Fi took the clear, glass bottle from the woman and pocketed it. "Thank you, but no, I didn't. I'm Fiona Blair and I work for the Magical Liaison Office. I understand you know about the piskies…"

Demelza studied the ID that Fi held out and drew herself up to her full height, her braided hair bobbing as she straightened her spine. "My dear, I am the author of 'Piskies; pest or persecuted'. Ask me anything."

Chapter 16

"You're aware that someone died from a piskie attack…"

Demelza's lip wobbled before her face hardened. "A terrible tragedy, but they can be territorial and if some idiot wandered near a nest…"

"There was nothing about a nest in the report. Any idea why the piskies might attack people?"

Demelza's smile turned icy. "I really have no idea. They could be aggravated by the invasion of their territory; they were here first you know."

"But tourists come to Cornwall every year, why attack now?"

"There have been some odd weather patterns lately, maybe climate change is impacting their internal equilibrium." Her demeanour moved from icy to arctic.

Fi made a note on her phone. If it was climate change then she was screwed, but her gut, and the fairy stones, said this was something else.

"The weather affects them?"

"The weather can have an impact on us all. Look outside."

Fi peered through the warped glass window at the scale-like clouds.

"A mackerel sky. It means change is on the way."

"O...K..." Fi ignored the folklore and got back to her questions. "Have you heard of a fairy stone?"

"Of course, I've got a few in stock. There."

Fi turned and her jaw dropped. "You keep an entire tub of magic stones?"

Demelza laughed. "They're not magic. You can find them anywhere around here, some people think they are a charm of protection, others that they are a type of fae currency, which is nonsense, of course. Everyone knows that star stones and maple syrup are the fae currencies of choice."

Fi didn't know that, but she made a note of it on her phone before approaching the plastic container with caution. She waved her hand over the box of stones, biting her lip as she concentrated. No magic hummed from the pile of pebbles, but she caught strange sensations from other parts of the shop.

"Do you have a licence to sell enchanted products?"

Demelza's broad face became pinched, and the atmosphere chilled further. She rooted around behind the counter before slapping a piece of paper on the polished surface. Fi squinted at it in the dim light and turned on her phone torch to confirm it was a valid licence. She snapped a picture and then hesitated. Was that sticky brush at the back of her teeth a sign of fae magic?

"Have you got fae magic in here?"

Demelza pointed up to a dream catcher with a smooth, circular pebble woven in the centre of the colourful threads. "I did a favour for a fae, and she gave me this in return. It's meant to bring luck and prosperity. I don't know if it works, but I've never had to pay a bill late since I got it."

"What favour did you do?"

"That's between me and her." Demelza lowered her dark eyebrows and Fi got the message.

"Do you know of any sinister uses for fairy stones?" Mort asked, leaning against the counter and giving the owner a winning smile to de-escalate things.

"Hmmph. There have been rumours, of course. From the olden times, mind, not recently. What was the story?" Demelza tapped her chin and then ambled to another part of the shop where large books were crammed into a rickety bookcase. She grabbed one, shook her head, then pulled another. "Ah, here we are." One knobbly finger tapped at a page. "This story talks about a fae who enchanted the stones to capture humans. Nonsense o'course. Fae stones don't have much power over humans. Now, hag stones are another matter…and, here, Professor hoity-toity Peter Rowlings thinks that fairy stones are the remnants of curses from long ago, left here by evil fae."

"And you disagree with him?"

"Course I do. Fae aren't evil by nature, they're different to humans, but there are good ones and not so good ones. Just like with people."

"So, you're saying people are people, even if they're fae?"

"Exactly. Fae, mermaid, people are the same. Most of 'em just want a safe place to call home and a quiet life. You can't blame 'em for that." Demelza's face crinkled into a smile and Fi felt like they'd rebuilt some trust.

"Mermaids?"

"Merpeople is the more politically correct term. There's a colony that lives along the coast. They don't get on with the fae, I've been trying to get to the bottom of why for my next book, but I haven't made much progress."

An image of a pale hand snatching a stone just above the dark sea made Fi bite her lip. "How could I talk to a mermaid?"

Demelza scoffed. "They're very shy, don't like to talk, but here." She scrawled a mark on a postcard and passed it over. "This is where I go to talk to them. Maybe you'll get lucky, but I talk more with fae than merfolk."

Fi took the postcard.

"Thanks. And you really have no idea why a fae would want to attack tourists?"

Demelza held up her hands. "I don't know. But I will say, they've lived here longer than we have and we're the ones trespassing. Now, if you don't have any more questions, I've got a shop to run. That'll be 50p for the postcard."

Fi turned slowly, taking in the empty shop. She knew a dismissal when she heard it. "OK," she said brightly, "I guess we're done here, for now." She pulled out her phone to pay for the card.

"Cash only under five pounds." Demelza tapped a handwritten sign proclaiming the same thing.

"Er…" Fi made the pantomime of searching for cash she knew she didn't carry. "Maybe I could just take a photo of the map."

"Here." Mort placed a shiny fifty pence piece on the counter. Her hero. With that, she grabbed the postcard, scooped up Cressida and swept out of the door. Or she would have swept, if the door hadn't opened the other way.

"It's pull."

"Yeah, got it, thanks." She left the shop with Mort following behind. "Oh," Fi popped her head back in, "and if you talk to any fae, could you tell them that if the piskies don't stop attacking people, they'll get exterminated." The door banged shut.

"That went well."

"You think so?" Fi asked.

"She seemed nice, and she gave you that cream for Cressida."

"I don't know, I've got a bad feeling about her."

"You get bad feelings about people who don't know how to use their phones."

"Yeah, well, it's not that hard."

"What's the plan now then?"

Fi spied a café opposite the shop. "How about a Cornish cream tea?"

Chapter 17

Fi snagged the table by the window and angled her chair so she could see Demelza's shop while Mort ordered. There was something odd about that woman. Maybe anyone who ran that type of curiosity shop was a bit weird, but Demelza hadn't seemed too bothered about the attacks.

Mort set the tray down on the table with a clatter. "One coffee and one tea. And the lady at the counter said that the Cornish way is jam first." He placed a small jar of strawberry jam and a tub of clotted cream next to the plates.

"What do you think they'd do to us if I went cream first?"

"I think we'd be chased out of the county. Best not to risk it."

Fi laughed and smeared jam onto the warm, fluffy scone. "Mmmm."

"Not as good as your scones, but nice."

Suck up.

"What are you saving up your brownie points for, Dr De'ath?"

"I'm sure something will come to mind."

Fi returned his slow smile and sipped her coffee. Delicious. Her phone rang, interrupting the cosy peace of the coffee shop.

"Hello?"

"Is that Fiona Blair?"

"Speaking."

"It's Dr Lowes from the coroner's office."

"Oh, right. Thanks for calling."

"I've emailed over the report, but I wanted to ring as well."

"OK."

"The man, identified as Brian Rossell, died of blood loss from multiple lacerations all over his face, neck, arms and legs. There's a lot of bruising, but no broken bones."

"And it was piskies?"

"Yes, the bites and claw marks are consistent with our records of piskie attacks."

"So, this has happened before?"

"Never as much as this summer, from what my colleagues at the hospital tell me, but every so often someone will wander into a piskie nest by accident. They don't normally kill – this is the first death I've seen and I've worked here for over twenty years – but they bite and scratch until the person leaves their territory. I've attached a couple of historic reports that I used for comparison."

"Thank you." The doctor seemed to be waiting for something else. "Very thorough."

"Yes, well, it's not often we get someone from the Magical Liaison Office down here to investigate anything, I want to make sure you've got everything you need." He sounded breathless.

"Thank you," Fi repeated, unsure what else to say. If her investigation counted as excitement then he needed to get out more. "There haven't been any other deaths, have there?"

"From piskies? No, thank goodness. You'll see from the pictures, but it was a brutal attack, hardly any skin left on his face, poor man."

"OK, I get the idea. And nothing else suspicious about any other deaths recently?"

"Nothing. Just the run of the mill stuff; car accidents, people falling off cliffs, the usual unfortunate accidents that happen every year. But I'll let you know if something else comes up."

"Thank you. I'll call if I've got any questions after I've read the report."

She checked her phone. No internet. "Fancy a walk?"

"Don't we have to work on the piskie case?"

Fi swallowed a mouthful of coffee. "Er, I need to get some internet to read the report."

"Right. A romantic walk to find an internet signal. Let's go."

They scoffed the cream tea and headed onto the small High Street.

"Sorry," Fi said.

"For what?"

"This holiday, it's not exactly a romantic getaway, is it? And you don't get much time away from the practice, and my job is ruining your down time."

"Come on, I'm enjoying spending time with you, and it's kind of fun to see you in action and be part of this. I mean, not the murder. Obviously. That's not fun, it's tragic." Fi smiled; it was refreshing to see the doctor fumbling for words. "Besides, if we solve it, we'll be heroes."

"Heroes?"

Mort nodded. "Of course, we'll have saved an entire species from a cull. Sounds pretty heroic to me."

Fi smiled; she hadn't thought of it like that.

I don't know why you want to save those creatures after they attacked you.

"Come on, Cress, where's your charitable spirit? Besides, they weren't acting under their own free will."

The wyrm flicked her tongue. *How many times? My name is Cressida.*

Fi's reply was interrupted by her phone buzzing. She finally had signal at the end of the High Street, next to a sign that asked people to clear away their dog mess. Ignoring the smell emanating from the poo bin, she clicked on alert.

"Fifty thousand!"

"What?"

"Oh, views."

Of what? Cressida flicked her tail.

"Of you." Fi winced and bent down to scratch her familiar behind her ear. "Look, I'm sorry, I'll tell them to take it down."

Wait, what was that comment?

"The one that says you're an exquisite specimen or the one that asks if you'll do requests for poses."

Cressida preened. *I suppose I can allow people to bask in my glory. Say thank you.*

"That's not how it works with comments…"

Nonsense. It's polite.

Fi rolled her eyes and typed out a comment that the wyrm said 'thank you' before getting off the app and opening the email from the coroner. She scanned the report before handing her phone to Mort. He read it and nodded.

"Death by blood loss caused by multiple lacerations."

Fi took back her phone and opened one of the pictures. The scone in her stomach did a flip as she took in the body. She showed it to Mort. "You still sure you want to get involved with this? You can go back to the cottage and chill."

He swallowed. "I'm sure we need to stop it. What's next?"

Fi looked beyond the red bin to the coast. "Let's go find a mermaid."

Chapter 18

Mort pulled up in a layby and Fi got out. She gazed at the sea. It was the bluest blue she had ever seen, fresher than the piskies' skin, deeper than the sky. Light sparkled off it as the waves caught the sun, reflecting like jewels on the summer's day.

Fi took Mort's hand and started down the dirt path that led down the cliff. The crisp tang of salt and the faint smell of fish filled her nostrils as they strolled down the path. Wavy grass stung Fi's hand, but the smile stayed on her face. She closed her eyes and inhaled.

When they reached the sand, Fi paused and unlaced her converse trainers, allowing her toes to sink into the sand. It felt grounding. Cressida, on the other hand – or should that be, claw? – picked her feet up, trying to avoid contact with the sand which stuck to the cream coating her body.

Ugh. Pick me up. I'll get sand in my scales.

Fi lifted Cressida onto her shoulders, grumbling about the ointment smearing her favourite hoody, hooked her shoes in her left hand and linked her other hand with Mort's again. This was…nice. A warm breeze played around them, and Fi felt her heart lighten. She felt content. That was it. She smiled up at Mort.

Another day, she'd suggest they walk along a beach together, maybe at sunrise…no… sunset. That was a normal couple thing to do, right? And maybe she could tell him how she felt…how she had fallen for him hard but couldn't admit it out loud in case she messed something up. She shook her head from her mundane fantasy and squinted around the cove. They were here for a reason.

"So, where should we look for this mermaid?" Mort asked.

"The sea is probably a good place to start."

"Ha, ha."

Fi scanned the small beach. Yellow-white sand gave way to black rocks on the other side. She pointed and Mort nodded.

As they got closer, Fi saw the rocks were more a dark green and brown with splashes of slimy seaweed than they were black. And there was one that angled slightly, almost like a bed. The perfect rock for someone to lie on. This had to be the place. But how to summon a mermaid?

Fi turned to technology and let go of Mort's hand to pull out her phone. No signal. Again. Bloody Cornwall. How could anywhere be so remote that it didn't have 4G in the twenty-first century. She'd even take 3G. But no. She waved her phone around. Nothing.

"Try calling her."

"How? I don't have a signal, or her phone number. If mermaids even have phones…"

"I meant, call her by talking towards the sea."

A blush crept up Fi's face. Sometimes she was so stupid. She hoped Mort put her flush down to the bracing sea air as she stepped forward and coughed. "Mermaid. Merlady…person. My name is Fiona Blair from the Magical Liaison Office and I need to talk to you about piskies."

Try putting your head under water.

Was that a joke? Fi twisted her head, trying to look her familiar in the eye, but Cressida kept a straight face as only a reptile can. Fine. Fi knelt on the smooth rock, the only surface not covered with bumpy barnacles, took a deep breath and plunged her head underwater.

Cressida yelped and leapt from Fi's shoulders as the cold sea touched her tail.

I didn't say drown me!

Fi smiled. Teach her right for stupid suggestions. She surfaced and said as much to the wyrm. Cressida turned her back on Fi and slunk over to Mort, who picked her up and cradled the wyrm, shooting a look of amusement at Fi.

"Did you talk to the mermaid?"

Right. She'd forgotten to say anything. "Give me a minute." She ducked her head under again and spoke, air bubbles frothing from her mouth in time with the words. "Mermaid. I need to speak to you. Please."

She resurfaced, brushing her soaking hair from her eyes, and stared across the shimmering water. What was she supposed to do now?

"Maybe send some magic out there. They might sense that more easily. Sharks can sense electric pulses, right?"

Fi frowned at her hands. "I'm not sure mermaids are like sharks…" But it couldn't hurt. She reached for her power, feeling the familiar flare as it crackled inside her. "Cressida, can you help? I don't want to kill anything by mistake."

Of course. Even though you tried to drown me, I'll help you out whenever you need it.

Fi narrowed her eyes at the golden wyrm and her sugar sweet voice. She focused until she felt the small internal click that was the familiar bond and siphoned some of her magic into the wyrm. Cressida's tongue sparked, and Mort adjusted his grip, so his bare skin didn't touch her scales as Fi's power filled her familiar.

Allowing the barest trickle of electricity to coat her hand, Fi tapped the surface of the water and willed her magic into the Atlantic ocean.

"Did it work?" Mort asked.

Fi shrugged her shoulders. Maybe she needed more power. She upped the wattage of her magic and tried again, this time sending a blast of electricity into the water.

Ripples bubbled through the waves. Fi smiled. It had worked. A large fin cut through the surface, heading straight for them. Fi stepped back. A dark shape approached. What had Mort said about sharks? Fi backed up some more until she was on the edge of the rock. How far could sharks jump?

With an explosion of spray, the mermaid burst from the waves and skidded along the smooth rock, water rippling over her skin.

Chapter 19

"Alright. You didn't need to shock me. I was on my way." The mermaid shook her head and rubbed the raised bumps that tattooed her temples in whorls. "I'll feel that all afternoon." She eyed the witch with bright pink eyes that reminded Fi of coral in nature documentaries. "I've never met a witch with electric magic."

"I guess I'm unique." Fi wiped the salty spray from her eyes and gazed at the beautiful creature lying before her.

Uniquely impertinent, Cressida snapped from the safety of Mort's arms. Fi shot her a look but didn't respond, and went back to staring at the figure on the rock.

The mermaid's skin rippled in mauves and turquoises as she stretched out on the rock. Her body was about the same size and shape as an average person. Fi's eyes found the mermaid's naked breasts through her thick grey-blue hair, well, maybe above average in some areas. The witch hugged her chest self-consciously.

Any similarities to a human ended at the creature's waist, where, instead of hips, her body swelled into a large tail that was double the length of her torso. The mermaid's tail lapped lazily against the waves, but it wasn't covered in fishy scales like Fi expected, instead it was smooth and coloured in bands of purple, lilac and cerulean as it tapered into the water, where a gigantic fin fanned out.

The mermaid's eyes sparkled as she watched Fi study her and her lips curved up. Fi coughed, uncomfortable being the source of the water maid's amusement. "I'm Fiona – Fi – Blair, and I wanted to talk to you about the piskies."

"I know. I heard. That's why I came, Fi Blair. But how did you know to find me here?"

"Demelza Zennor showed me a map."

The mermaid hissed. "She's no friend of ours. She doesn't understand that we don't want attention. The more humans know about us, the worse it is for our kind. Best to stay as a half-forgotten myth and keep out of the way of the fishing boats."

"Was it you? At Tintagel castle?" Fi squinted as the mermaid shifted, sending rays of reflected sunlight into her eyes.

The sea maid let out a sigh which sounded like a melody. "It was. My family have been monitoring the coastlines ever since Joan started stirring things up again. I saw you find this." With a flick of her wrist, the fairy stone appeared in the mermaid's hand, and she offered it to the witch. Fi took it, her fingers brushing the thin webbing that stretched between the mermaid's fingers.

"It's safe. Fairy magic doesn't work in salt water so now it's just a trinket."

"Who's Joan?" Fi latched onto the name.

"Joan the Wad as she likes to be known. She's the piskie queen."

"And she's the one behind all of this. Why?"

"Who knows how piskies think? Every couple of hundred years or so, she tries to get a foothold back in the county. It makes trouble for other supernaturals; humans don't like being attacked and they take it out on all of us. But there's not a lot we can do seeing as all the attacks happen on land."

A shout pulled Fi's attention from the water. A couple waved down from the coastal path, pointing at the mermaid. The sea creature frowned, lines crinkling her perfect brow, making the small bumps along it stand out more.

The sea spray foamed up and morphed into tendrils of fog that partially clouded the beach from view, but Fi saw the people start down the coastal path. They didn't have long and she still had questions.

"Mermaids can't leave the water then?"

"I'm not a selkie!"

"Alright, sorry. No offense meant."

The mermaid settled back down on the rock as the couple passed from sight. "None taken. It's bad enough when the humans accidentally encounter us, but if they start hunting supernaturals again…"

"That was hundreds of years ago…"

The mermaid's bright eyes burned into Fi. "Doesn't mean that history can't repeat itself."

"I'm trying to stop this. How can I find Joan?"

"She lives in the fae realm and there's a portal in Cornwall."

"OK…where?"

"No idea. It's not along the coast, or my family would have felt it."

Fi spun the circular pebble on one finger. There couldn't be that much of Cornwall not next to the sea, so that narrowed it down. She hoped.

"If you do manage to get through, don't trust in anything they say. Fae are a tricky folk, but Joan the Wad is the queen of illusions, she's a will o' wisp, loves leading travellers astray. You can't trust your senses around a fae. And do not bargain with them or enter into any sort of agreement. You do not want to owe any fae a favour, believe me."

Fi wanted to ask what the mermaid had agreed to that caused the bitterness in her voice, but the sea creature's eyes flicked up, focusing on something behind Fi. The couple re-emerged halfway down the cliff path, heading for the small beach.

"I'd better go. If anyone else spots me here, it'll become a tourist trap and I'll lose my favourite cove. And if you do find Joan, you'd better have a translator. Grandad says she only speaks old Cornish…"

"Thank you. Wait, what's your name?" Fi called after the mermaid as she disappeared into the waves with a small splash.

"Nerissa." The reply floated over the foamy sea.

"Did you see a mermaid?" A man in a brown jacket pushed past Fi and stood on the rock, staring out at the waves.

"Nope. Probably just a dolphin or a seal."

"Are you sure, it looked like you were talking with someone…"

Fi shook her head. "Must have been a trick of the light."

She squinted at the headland where a dark swarm of piskies massed around a figure before disappearing.

"OK…hey, is that a wyrm?" He headed for Cressida, who bared her sharp teeth at his outstretched hand.

"I wouldn't touch her; she's got scale rot. Could be contagious."

How dare you!

The man pulled his hand back with a start. "Oh. Right, sorry. We'll get back to it then, got another couple of miles to the local pub." The tourists walked off.

Fi shrugged at her familiar. "Got them to leave you alone, didn't I? And we've got some more information. Did you see someone with the piskies up there?"

Where?

"Let's get back to the café and I'll look up this Joan the Wad."

They made it to Mort's car before Fi's phone blared. She stared at the screen alert.

"Change of plans. We've got to get to Land's End. Now!"

Chapter 20

"Which way is that?"

"No idea." Fi fumbled with the car's built in sat nav and found the tourist spot. The wheel of waiting turned on the screen as it recalculated the route and Fi tapped her foot as she waited.

Can you stop that? I'm trying to sleep back here, now it finally doesn't itch.

"I have to do something. There!" Fi pointed at the screen, causing Mort to swerve the car. He cursed and regained control as they hurtled towards a bush.

"I can't turn round here!"

Fi stared up at the hedge that loomed higher than Mort's four by four along the lane. There weren't any passing places and the track was barely wide enough for his large car, let alone to turn around and Fi had no idea what on earth were they meant to do if they met an oncoming vehicle.

"Just keep going then, it'll reprogram itself soon." Fi clenched her hands into fists and kept them on her lap. Her instinct was to fiddle with the sat nav, but if she lost control of her power, she might blow the car battery and then they'd go nowhere.

Calm yourself. I can't sleep with you fussing.

Fi was about to tell her familiar where she could go sleep when Mort spoke. "Why are we going to Land's End?"

She glanced at the doctor. Mort hurtled the car down the narrow roads, and Fi turned her face to the screen grateful she didn't have to drive. His jaw tensed as he navigated the lane as quickly as he could, grimacing whenever a branch scraped his car. Shaking her head, she focused on the phone.

"Right. There's an attack, happening now. We have to get there and find the fairy stone before someone gets hurt." Fi cursed as the live stream of screeching piskies cut out. "Bloody internet down here." She gripped her phone and waved it around, as if that would somehow pick up a signal.

Through the sketchy connection, Fi monitored the situation as the car sped towards Land's End. No deaths. So far. The sat nav did indeed reprogramme itself once it realised they were ignoring it and got them back on some sort of main road, or at least not a road that looked like it might lead to another realm, and Mort accelerated. Mort skidded the car to a stop in a car park and they stared at the mega swarm circling around the cliff.

People crouched low in their cars, hiding away from the angry creatures, but there were others in bright cagoules fleeing down the coastal path.

"We have to help."

"OK." Mort swallowed. "What's the plan?"

"Protect the people and find the fairy stone. Try not to get killed."

He nodded. Fi paused, one hand on the door handle, and turned to Mort. She planted a kiss on his lips. "Don't get killed. Cressida, find that stone."

Chapter 21

Fi leapt from the car and charged towards the mass of blue piskies. "Stay close to me." Fi flung up a shield of electricity as the piskies shrieked and turned towards them. Mort's sword appeared in his hand, and he held it, ready to fight.

The piskies veered away from his blade and focused on Fi instead, crackling as they hit her shield. They forced their way through the mass of bug-like creatures to the nearest bright blob of colour. The man screamed as Mort placed a hand on his shoulder.

"It's alright, we're here to help."

The man turned large brown eyes to them, looking at Mort as if he were a knight in shining armour. Fi coughed. "Stay close to me."

With a grunt of effort, she extended her shield to cover the man. He gaped at the flickering blue electricity shimmering around them.

"Is this magic?"

"Yep."

He reached out a hand.

"Don't touch it!" How stupid could people be?

Idiot! Cressida hissed as she raced off to find the stone.

The man jerked his arm back. "Right. Of course not."

"What happened?"

"We were taking pictures when they came out of nowhere."

Fi winced as piskies slammed onto her shield, each of them fading into small popping crackles on her electricity. A blur of yellow caught her eye. Someone had curled up in a ball, right by the cliff edge and piskies swarmed round them.

"Get in a car. I'm going to help them."

"But I don't have a…"

"Get in any car!"

Fi ran as the man yanked open the nearest, thankfully unlocked, car door and clambered in. Piskies crashed into the glass, knocking the car and denting the paintwork, but he was safe.

The teenager screamed and cradled her head, pushed back towards the edge by the mass of creatures. Fi aimed an arc of electricity overhead, driving the piskies away.

"Get up. Run," she shouted.

The girl pushed herself up. Her foot slipped on the loose dirt and her mouth formed a small 'o' as she fell backwards. Fi dived for the teenager's hand, barely feeling the rocks that scraped her skin as she skidded along the ground. She grasped the girl's hand and braced.

"Climb back up," she panted, unsure how long she could hold the screaming girl. The teenager twisted and shrieked, dangling over the cliff edge, ignoring Fi. The witch let a small trickle of electricity flow into the girl's hand. It shocked the teenager into silence, and she stared up at Fi with wide eyes. "Please, you have to climb up."

The teenager stopped squirming and reached for a tuft of grass on the cliff face. She pulled herself up, kicking at the rock with her feet as she levered herself back to safety. Fi pulled, lending her strength to the girl. In her exertion, she dropped the shield and sharp piskie claws pricked into her legs and arms.

Fi swore as more of the creatures grabbed onto her and before she could get up a shield, they hoisted her into the air. Fi kept her grip on the girl, now dangling above the clifftop.

Sure the teenager was far enough from the edge, Fi let go and the girl landed with a thump.

"Run for a car!" Fi shouted.

The teenager fled, her hair bobbing and arms flailing as she batted at the few piskies who followed her. Fi sent a bolt of lightning out, clearing the girl's path. The witch twisted in the grip of dozens of tiny, clawed hands as they drew her up. Enough. Fi flared her magic through her body, and the salt air filled with the smell of burning hair and skin. The piskies screeched and dropped her.

Fi screamed as she plummeted to the ground. She landed hard. Shaking her head, she re-created her shield of electricity and stared around.

“Where are you, Cressida?”

Chapter 22

Fi scanned the cliff top and found a hint of gold at the base of a white signpost that marked out that this was Land's End and showed distances to other destinations in neat black print. Everywhere else was bloody far away.

I've found the stone. Despite the distance, Cressida's voice sounded clear in Fi's mind.

Fi sprinted towards her familiar, who's body crackled with their shared magic, shielding her from the attacking piskies. She slid to a stop, her shoes throwing dust up around them.

Cressida sneezed, sending a small fireball towards Fi's feet. *There,* she said through a mouth full of dust and snot.

Fi felt through the dust cloud until her fingers grasped the smooth, round pebble. Like the one from Tintagel Castle, this had a perfect circle cut through the centre. Now all she had to do was get it in the water.

The piskies' chattering increased in volume as they flung themselves at the witch. Fi felt her magic falter. She had used too much power too quickly. She pocketed the stone and looked around wildly, seeking salt water to dull its power over the piskies. The closest was over the cliff, but the piskies darted around, seeking holes in her weak magic.

Mort lunged in front of Fi, spinning his sword, keeping the piskies at bay. But there were thousands, and they swooped around his silver blade, sharp claws scramming any exposed skin.

Fi drew her magic back from the familiar bond and stuffed Cressida inside her top, protecting the small wyrm with her own body. Her shield buzzed for a second then flickered again as the piskies rammed it.

"I need more power!" Fi screamed. Why did they have to be in the middle of nowhere? No buildings. No pylons. Nothing she could siphon power from…except…

She reached a hand towards the carpark, stretching out her fingers as she willed the stored power from over thirty vehicle batteries to her aid. Electricity arced through the air to her in differing strengths as she drained the power. Two bright blue bolts slammed into her chest and she absorbed the electricity, swallowing hard as the sparky taste of her magic filled her mouth and nostrils. Thank goodness for electric car batteries.

Humming with her newfound power, Fi sent out a wave of electricity, forcing the fae creatures back long enough for her to sprint for the edge. She flung the fairy stone as far as she could and sent a bolt of electricity after it, stopping any of the piskies from grabbing the rock before it sank into the water.

With a faint splash, the fairy stone disappeared into the sea and the piskies' chattering lessened. Fi swatted at one that flew too close. It gnashed its pointed teeth but flew off, and others followed, unconcerned with injuring humans now that the magic of the stone wasn't forcing them to act.

Fi turned with a smile. Another fairy stone neutralised. Then her eyes lit on Mort, panting on the ground.

She ran over and cradled his head. Blood streamed from the myriad of tiny cuts across his face and neck.

"We need to get you to a hospital." Fi hauled him upright and slung her arm around his waist.

"I'm fine. Just get the first aid kit." He tried to brush her off, but she clung to him, dread curling in her heart. She had decided to take the case on their romantic getaway, and now he was hurt. Her own grazes forgotten, she led them back to the car and left Mort leaning on the door while she grabbed the first aid kit from the boot.

Her hands shook as she fumbled with the catch on the green plastic case, but she had it open. What now? She stared down at the sealed packages and bottles of potions that she didn't recognise. What was he planning for when he'd packed this?

"Antiseptic wipes first."

Right. Of course. Wipes. Because he was hurt. Because of her.

Pass him the wipes. Cressida's voice cut through the fog in Fi's mind and she took the entire box to where Mort stood, peering into the wing mirror as he assessed his cuts. Fi handed him the wipes and bit her lip as he winced from the sting of the antiseptic.

He'll be OK. He's a doctor.

Fi nodded, but her hands twitched at her side, unable to keep still but not knowing what to do to help. Mort stared at the mirror as he cleaned the wounds, then applied gauze stitches to the larger cuts.

A call behind her made her turn.

"What are we supposed to do now?"

Fi frowned. "Go home…or back to your hotels. Enjoy your holiday. And maybe stay out of the tourist hotspots until I can figure out how to stop this Joan the Wad."

The speaker blinked at her. "I meant, what are we supposed to do now that you've fried our cars."

"Oh." Blood rushed to Fi's face, then she frowned again, deepening the wrinkles in her forehead. "I didn't fry the cars. They still work." She hoped. "I just borrowed the power."

"Well give it back. None of them will turn on."

A man in a lime green Volkswagen van with purple trim turned the key in his ignition to prove the point.

"I can't give it back. I used it on the piskies. To save you." Anger bubbled in Fi's chest, the last of her magic worming its way to the surface. "And all you care about is your stupid cars? Mort could have been killed!"

Calm down.

"You're lucky I was here, or you'd be dead." A hand patted her arm and she whirled, the remains of her power crackling to her fingertips.

"I'm not dead, but it's nice that you care." Mort grinned at her, plasters and stitches covering his face, and Fi's face went from tomato to beetroot red. "Now, how about you reassure these people, Agent Blair?"

Fi stared at him. She shouldn't need him to remind her that she was a Magical Liaison Office Community Agent. She should not lose her cool. She coughed and turned back to the crowd. What would her boss do?

"I work for the Magical Liaison Office, so please direct all enquiries to their hotline. The threat has been neutralised, but I recommend you avoid popular tourist spots until the piskie crisis is over. As to your cars, they'll require charging so I suggest you call whatever roadside assistance you have and ask them to bring enough battery packs to jump start the cars. That will be all."

Too right. You saved their lives and they're complaining about their stupid cars.

"I know, right?"

Humans are unbelievable.

"For sure." With a toss of her dishevelled ponytail, she climbed into the car and calmed her breathing.

Well done. You told them, ungrateful idiots.

"Thanks, Cressida." It was nice to have the wyrm on her side. She turned to Mort. "Are you really alright?"

"I will be."

Her brow puckered. "I still think you should go to the hospital."

Mort shook his head. "I'm not spending hours in A&E so they can send me home with stitches. Trust me, I'm a doctor."

Fi raised one eyebrow. "Fine. But you're not driving back." Mort rolled his eyes and Fi continued, "I'm serious. You've had multiple head injuries. There's no way you'd let me drive in that condition."

He hesitated and Fi held her hand out for the keys.

"Maybe you're right. My vision is a little blurred and I don't know if *Cure All* works on head injuries… But you're hurt too."

"Nothing serious." Fi's side blared in pain as the adrenaline faded from her system, but it was the fiery burn of a graze. She'd had worse. It wasn't like she'd been hit in the chest with a bolt of magic, or clouted by a giant pumpkin vine. She winced as the painful memories rose. Mort took that as a sign she was really injured and bent over to examine her side through the tear in the shirt.

Fi batted him away. "It's nothing. Just pass me the *Cure All*, best not to risk you drinking it, the taste alone might make you puke." Fi slugged the fiery aniseed drink and soothing warmth filled her. Thank goodness for Madam Mim's potion. "Right. I'm driving."

Mort got out of the car, putting the stopper back in the *Cure All*, and Fi slid over. She adjusted the chair and checked the mirrors. The crowd milled around, holding their phones out to get a signal. Lucky she hadn't fried their devices as well when she'd drained the electricity. A couple of them waved their arms in agitation, but most were calm. One family even spread a picnic blanket and tucked into a plate of sausage rolls as if they hadn't just witnessed an animal attack. Tourists were weird.

"I'm still not sure this is a good idea."

"Look, either I drive us back or we wait here for an ambulance. Your choice, doc."

Mort sighed. "OK, you drive."

Chapter 23

Fi siphoned the remains of her power into Mort's car battery. She clutched the steering wheel as the car inched forward.

Go.

She accelerated then braked sharply as another car zoomed past. She gripped the steering wheel until her knuckles turned white. Fi shook her head. She had lost her nerve, and they weren't even out of the car park yet.

That was your gap.

"Since when do you know about driving?" Fi hissed.

I know the car has to actually move forwards to be considered 'driving'.

"You're no help." Fi finally made the turn and followed the sat nav's directions, pulling out onto another too narrow country lane. A hedge loomed on one side in parallel to the cutting edges of the stone wall that lined the road on the other side as it twisted and turned through the Cornish countryside.

Mort's head lolled to one side, and he let out a soft snore. He'd fallen asleep ten minutes into the journey. Fi drummed her fingers on the steering wheel. Did that mean he had a concussion? She turned the radio up even louder.

You tried that already. It didn't help. Turn it down before you get pulled over for breach of peace.

With a sigh, Fi pressed at the buttons on the steering wheel and turned the volume down on her second attempt. Blasting soft rock probably wasn't the way to wake someone up, and she couldn't connect her phone to the car to get some heavy metal music playing without stopping the car…and if she stopped the car, she wasn't sure she could force herself to get it going again.

Watch out for that post.

"What?" Fi swerved to avoid the sign. Her hands tightened on the wheel. What was she thinking? She couldn't drive. A horn blared behind her and she snuck a look in the rear view mirror but refused to speed up. The tractor beeped again.

"Alright, alright. I hear you. You're a bloody tractor, why can't you drive in the field?"

A car approached on the other side of the road and Fi squealed. She pulled as tight to the bushes as she dared and held her breath as it passed.

You know it doesn't make the car thinner when you hold your breath.

"If you haven't got anything helpful to say then you can shut up or it'll be your fault when we crash and burn."

At five miles an hour, the most you'll do is dent the car.

"I said be quiet."

After an age, Fi pulled into the long driveway at the holiday cottage and turned off the engine. She slumped against the leather seats, her breath coming easily at last.

Mort stretched and opened his eyes. "Here already? Well done."

He got out of the car and wobbled a little. Fi stopped gaping and ran to support him. "Take it easy. Let's get you inside."

She felt him stiffen and looked up. Fi followed his gaze to the large scratch down the paint work of his car.

"Sorry," she said.

He waved it off but kept glancing at the car as he shambled to the cottage.

She gave a half-hearted wave to the landlady's father who waved back with equal enthusiasm before he turned back to topping up the milk in the dish on the ground.

Fi flung the door open and helped Mort to the sofa. "Are you sure you don't need to go to the hospital? What if you've got concussion?"

"All they'll do is monitor me anyway. It's better to be home. You talk to me and I'll be fine." He winced as he moved his head.

Fi scrabbled in the freezer for anything she could use as an ice pack and came out with a bag of out-of-date frozen peas clutched in her hand. She wrapped it in a tea towel and handed it to Mort.

"Here, put this on your head."

"Yes, doctor." Mort's lips tilted up in a fuzzy smile.

"None of that. You're injured."

"I can think of some things you could do to make me feel better."

Fi danced away and pulled out her phone, searching for treatments for head injuries. "Nope. It says here that you need to rest. Is there any clear fluid coming from your ears?"

Mort put his hand to his ear and tapped it. "Nope. I told you, I'm fine."

Fi span out of his grip. "Rest! I'll make you something to eat. Unless you're feeling nauseous. Are you feeling sick?"

"I'm fine! Sit down."

Fi sat and fidgeted. "Let's play a game." She rooted around in a cupboard until she found a board game.

"Scrabble? That's a bit unfair for someone who's got a head injury."

"Uno?"

"No, Scrabble's fine. I was joking."

"Ha. Ha."

Fi set out the tiles and Cressida jumped up beside her. *Vixen. 30 points on that double word score.*

"Thank you. I can play myself. And how do you know how to play Scrabble?"

Goody and I used to play all the time. She was a canny wordsmith. Cressida's emerald eyes turned wistful at the thought of her previous witch, and Fi felt the wave of love and grief flow through the familiar bond.

Fi gave her wyrm a reassuring pat on the head, laid the tiles and suppressed a smile at Mort's dismay. "Not fair. Two against one."

Chapter 24

Fi pulled out the mixing bowl carefully and placed it on the counter. Mort sat on the sofa, changing channels but Fi couldn't sit still. She glanced over every few seconds, checking he still breathed and hadn't collapsed. He might be blasé about his injuries, but Fi was worried.

She couldn't shake the crushing weight that filled her chest. This was her fault. They wouldn't have been in Land's End if she hadn't brought work with her on this holiday. All he'd wanted was some quiet time away. Just the two of them. And she couldn't even do that.

She searched for sugar.

It's not your fault, you know that.

"Huh?"

I can feel your guilt like a lead weight through the bond. It wasn't you. It was the piskies.

"Yeah, and how did we get involved with the piskies?"

Were you honestly going to ignore the problem and let an entire species get exterminated so you could enjoy your holiday?

"No...but they still might. I haven't found this Joan the Wad."

Then why are you baking instead of looking?

"Because I need something to do!" Fi glanced at Mort and lowered her voice as a soft snore came from the sofa. Mort had fallen asleep. Again. "I'm worried about him, OK? And I don't know what to do, and it's scary and awful and...I care about him so much."

That's what happens when you love someone. But it's part of life and you're no good to anyone if you're worrying. Cressida paused, her tongue flicking out as she met Fi's gaze. *Besides, if you want to cook something, I could go for a nice sausage.*

Fi let out a half laugh, half sob. She wiped her eyes and got out a frying pan alongside the baking equipment. "Fine. I'll make you something. But, can you watch Mort while I get make a quick trip to the shops?"

Cressida coughed. Fi turned, unused to subtlety from the wyrm, but she could feel a hint of curiosity through their shared bond.

How's the photo doing?

"Sorry, I forgot to take it down. I'll sort it."

No, I mean, how many views does it have?

"Oh." Fi pulled out her phone. "Fifty thousand."

Cressida made a pleased sound in the back of her throat.

"Do you want me to get it taken down? I just need to message the group."

No. No, you can leave it up.

"Right. Well, keep an eye on Mort, OK?"

The wyrm nodded and Fi shrugged on a jacket and headed out. She nodded to the old man again, now crouched by the bowl of milk he'd poured. He crooned to something in his hand and Fi kept walking.

At the small shop in the village, she selected the ingredients she needed and picked up a pack of local sausages for her familiar. On the way back, she bumped into their landlady for the week. Tamsyn fell into step with Fi, cradling a pile of worn library books.

"Doing some shopping?"

"Yeah, I needed some sugar for scones."

"You should have popped by the house; I could have given you some."

"Thanks, but I got some other bits too. I wouldn't want to raid your freezer."

"So, how's the holiday going?"

"Er…" Fi wondered how she should answer. Somehow, the truth; that they'd been attacked by swarms of piskies – twice – and met a mermaid, and had to somehow find a way to either destroy all the fairy stones in Cornwall or convince Joan the Wad to back off, didn't seem like the right answer. "Yeah. It's good."

"You picked the right week for it. The weather's been great."

"There was that storm the other day…"

Tamsyn shrugged and rearranged the books in her arms. "It's always changeable down here, it's the sea and the magic so Da says."

"About your dad…"

"Oh no. What's he done now? I tell him that the cottage is for guests and to leave them alone, but he just can't help himself. He hasn't offered to take you fishing, has he?"

"No. He's just putting out bowls of milk…"

"That." Tamsyn let out a sigh of relief. "He's got this thing about being kind to the faeries here, so he leaves out a bowl of milk for them, thinks it brings good luck or something. A lot of the older people round here do it. And he found a piskie the other day…he decided to nurse it back to health. It knocked over three of the ornamental dogs before he got it in a bird cage. I said I didn't want it in the house, but he thinks it'll put him in good favour with Joan the Wad, whoever she is."

"Queen of the piskies," Fi said without thinking. "Wait. Your dad knows about Joan the Wad?"

"Why don't you ask him yourself?"

Tamsyn stopped by the steps to the larger house, where her dad continued to sing to something in his large, weather-beaten hands. As Fi moved closer, she could see the familiar dark blue of a piskie through his fingers.

"Da, Fiona wants to ask you about the piskies."

He looked up. "Wasun?"

"Er, what do you know about Joan the Wad?"

His reply made no sense to Fi and she looked to Tamsyn for help.

"He said she's a will o' the wisp, likes to lead travellers astray for fun, but she's fierce about protecting Cornwall and, if you treat her right, she'll bring good luck. That's why he leaves out the milk for her kin, the piskies."

"Any idea where she lives?"

Again Tamsyn smoothly played interpreter. "Out on the moors, in her realm. Who knows?"

"Thanks, that's really helpful."

"Anytime. And let me know if you need anything at all."

Fi promised that she would and headed into the holiday cottage. She stared at her boyfriend and familiar playing Scrabble. They'd worked out a system where Cressida flicked her tongue at the tiles she wanted to use for Mort to place them on the board before she pushed them into place with her claws.

"Who's winning?"

Shhhh. I'm trying to concentrate.

"I think she's cheating. What sort of a word is 'qis'?"

It's a word.

Fi searched on her phone. "She's right. It's a vital thought in Chinese philosophy."

Mort folded his arms and glared at the board.

"OK, I'll leave you to it, shall I?" Fi said.

Chapter 25

Fi mixed the ingredients for her scones. They wouldn't quite taste the same without the fae sugar she used at home, which made them so light and sweet, they were irresistible. But they'd still be tasty. And she wasn't sure she wanted to use fae sugar again after her experiences with the piskies. Were they involved in sugar manufacture? She had no idea.

More importantly, baking gave her something to do. She allowed her mind to wander as her hands went through the familiar motions of mixing, rolling, and cutting. What was she missing?

She knew who controlled the piskies but what did the mermaid mean about needing a translator? And, more pressing, where was Joan the Wad? It wasn't like she could just walk into the fae realm and ask. She shook her head and banged the tray of scones into the oven, followed by a second baking tray full of fat sausages.

Keep it down, will you?

The Scrabble game had grown competitive and the atmosphere around the table thrummed with tension from both man and wyrm. Mort let out a chuckle as he laid some tiles over a triple word score.

"Ha! There's an x in that. 36 points. Head injury, my arse!"

It's not his arse that's the problem.

Fi snorted but didn't repeat Cressida's sniping comment to Mort.

The wyrm let out a hiss of irritation and Fi could feel her annoyance through the familiar bond. They were fine. She left them to it and switched on her laptop. She pulled up the virtual corkboard and stared at it before adding in the latest attack.

Fi's phone rang and she answered the video call from her sister, sinking back onto the sofa next to Mort who had crossed his arms and looked smug. Fi could feel the irritation bubbling through the familiar bond as Cressida stared at her letters.

"Agatha? What's up?"

"Oh, hi Fi, I was just calling to check that you're coming back on Sunday."

"That's the plan."

"Good, good."

"What's wrong?"

"Hmm? Oh, nothing's wrong, it's just…" Agatha lowered her voice and looked around, "…Mum."

"Mum?"

"She's a total nightmare."

"What's she done now?" Fi sat bolt upright, a thousand scenarios of worse injuries running through her mind.

"What hasn't she done? I keep telling her to rest, but she insists on hobbling about the house doing things, then, when I try to do them for her, she stands there telling me how to do them. I know how to put on a washing machine for goddess' sake. And she's downed an entire bottle of *Cure All* under some delusion that she'll get better faster…"

"Did it work?"

"Of course it didn't work! It's a broken bone not a graze or a tickly cough!" Agatha pulled at a strand of her chestnut brown hair, winding it tightly around one finger.

"Just asking."

"She's got a fudging stick now, too. I had to stop her hitting Neville with it last night. He was only trying to help, but Mum couldn't believe that you put coffee granules in bolognaise…"

It took Fi a second to realise her sister wasn't actually talking about a stick for making fudge, but then she had to ask, "Coffee in tomato sauce? Seems like a waste of good coffee. Wait, you didn't use my Goblin Blend, did you?" Fi sided with her mum on this, frowning as she sank back against the cushions.

"It brings out the flavour. You'd think she'd be happy to experiment given how much she loves making those darn potions."

"Come on, Aggy, leg it go."

Her sister pursed her lips, trying not to smile as she replied with her own pun. "She's just being so slow to heel."

"Oh, very good, but not leg-endary."

"Pull the other leg."

"Too funny by calf."

"Legs-actly."

Fi shook her head and her sister groaned. Agatha had lost that pun battle, and she knew it.

"Is that Fi?" Their mother hobbled into the room, a black cane in her hand.

"Hi Mum."

"What has Agatha been saying?"

"I haven't said anything, I was just calling my sister."

"Hmph. Well things are going a lot better here now everyone's started listening to me. You enjoy the rest of your holiday, and we'll see you on Sunday."

"If I don't kill you by then…" Agatha muttered.

"What was that?"

"Bye Fi," her sister said brightly, before mouthing 'help me' at the camera.

Fi smiled and hung up. It sounded like things were back to normal at home if her mother was aggravating Agatha. Just as well, because they were no closer to solving the problematic piskies in Cornwall.

She turned back to her virtual board with a sigh, then her brain sparked with an idea. She needed a map.

Chapter 26

Fi pulled up a virtual map of Cornwall and dropped pins for every attack reported over the past month. There had to be a pattern; it couldn't be random. The first attacks were close together, Land's End was the farthest, then they spread out. So, maybe the piskie queen had grown in confidence and spread her reach.

Tamsyn's dad had said she lived on the moor, but there was a lot of open land in the middle of the first attacks. Joan the Wad could live anywhere.

Frustrated, she drummed one hand on the table and zoomed in on the map, searching for anything that might give her a clue.

Will you stop that incessant tapping?

"I'm looking for a lead."

I'm playing Scrabble.

Fi shook her head. The game between Mort and Cressida had reached new heights of tension as the letters ran lower and lower.

"Hah! I'm out…and that puts me in the lead."

"Congratulations."

He cheated.

"I'm sure Mort didn't cheat."

"Of course I didn't!"

He changed the scores.

"He wouldn't do that. Just accept your losses like a good wyrm. You can't win every time."

I demand a rematch. Cressida swiped half the tiles onto the floor with her tail and narrowed her eyes.

Fi eyed the darkening bags under Mort's eyes. "Maybe later. I think the patient needs to get some sleep."

"I'm fine." Mort's yawn undermined his protests. "But, maybe you're right. I could do with the rest."

Fi nodded and hovered as Mort stood and walked to the bedroom.

"I can get into bed by myself."

Fi forced herself to stop and instead stood, bobbing from foot to foot in the doorway. "You'll call me if you need anything?"

"Scout's honour." Mort did a wobbly three-fingered salute and climbed into bed.

Fi scowled. She hated feeling helpless and Mort's injuries weren't something she could solve. If he'd been a broken motherboard or a software issue, she might have a chance, but people were outside of her expertise.

With a sigh, she turned back to the open-plan living area and took the food out of the oven. Cressida hopped up onto the side, her forked tongue tasting the air as dribbles of drool formed at the side of her mouth.

"Wait for it to cool down or you'll hurt yourself."

The wyrm tsked and eyed the sausages that Fi heaped onto a plate.

Her phone rang again. She answered without bothering to check who it was.

"Agatha?"

"No. Agent Jones."

Fi jerked upright. "Oh, hi."

"I need a status report. Now. There's an emergency debate scheduled tomorrow. Some Members of Parliament are calling for complete extermination. One of the Scottish MPs claims piskies aren't even native to the UK. What have you found?"

Fi recapped what she knew about the fairy stones and the locations.

"Good work. Get that in a report asap. I might be able to head this off. What's your plan?"

Good question. "Er, the attacks seem to be concentrated in popular tourist destinations, so if I can neutralise all the stones then the piskies should stop attacking people."

"It solves the immediate problem, and might buy us some time, but someone's putting these artefacts in place. Who wants to cause problems to Cornwall's main industry and has access to fae magic?"

Another good question. "Not sure."

An alert pinged on her laptop and she stared at the words that scrolled across the screen. Fi swallowed. "Got to go. There's been another attack."

There was a long pause before Agent Jones replied. "Keep me informed and send me that report." She hung up and Fi clicked on the alert. She gasped at the picture that accompanied the article, of a place called Mên-an-Tol. A massive boulder shaped like a giant fairy stone filled the screen. And it was on the moors.

Chapter 27

Fi searched for Mên-an-Tol to double check she had the right place and dozens of images of a grey circular standing stone set between two smaller stones filled her screen, like an error 101 sign. But switching protocols didn't cause piskies to go crazy, and this wasn't as simple as coding. She clenched her hands into fists. This had to be the gateway to Joan the Wad's realm and how she entered their world.

She tapped one finger against the keyboard. She had to go. But, Mort was ill and in bed. She couldn't leave him with head injuries. Her mind raced in time with the click clack of her finger on the plastic case.

You have to go.

"What? How can I leave Mort?"

He's fine. He's asleep. Nothing is going to happen here.

"But…"

If there's a chance you can save a species from the stupidity of humans, you have to do it.

"You were the one who said I shouldn't help them after they attacked us."

Sometimes I speak before I think.

Fi stared at Cressida. That was the closest she'd come to an apology for her cutting comments.

You have to stop this now. Why do you think wyrms are so rare? Humans captured us, skinned us for our glittering scales, ground our claws up for aphrodisiacs, and even our superiority couldn't save us against their cruel weapons.

"I never knew that."

Cressida sighed. *You wouldn't. The magical extinction act of 1862 saved my species, included us as a protected animal across the continent and then we became popular pets. The* wyrm spat out the word. *Most of my kind don't have the self-awareness that I do, but…you can't let the piskies down. They don't know what they're doing.*

"Are you sure?"

You saw them. They're scavengers trying to make their way in a changing world. Their queen is the one behind the attacks and she's going to get them all killed.

"But, Mort…" Fi glanced at the bedroom door. "You have to stay here."

I beg your pardon.

"Please, Cressida. Watch him, make sure he's OK. If anything happens…"

Nothing is going to happen.

"Then you can stay here."

I should be at your side, protecting you.

"You'll do more for me if I know he's safe."

There's nothing I can say that will change your mind, is there?

Fi shook her head. "If you don't stay here, I can't go."

Then it seems I have no choice. Cressida tsked. *Don't die.*

"I'm not planning on it."

And don't do anything stupid.

"I can't promise that."

Cressida's raspy laugh coursed through Fi's mind. The witch grinned, grabbed her phone and jacket, hesitate then scooped up Mort's keys before she headed outside. The old man's singing caught her ear. The mermaid had said she'd need a translator. And she wanted to delay getting into Mort's four by four.

"I don't suppose you want to meet Joan the Wad, do you?" It was half joke, half hope.

He stood and rubbed the back of his neck, making a sound like sandpaper. "Aye, be good t'un see eye."

Tamsyn stepped out of their door. "Not bothering you, is he?"

"No, I invited him on a road trip to see Joan the Wad."

"The piskie queen?"

"Fill you in on the way to Mên-an-Tol."

Tamsyn's face crinkled up. "But there's nothing there."

"Want to bet?"

"Alright, I'll bite, if Da wants to go…"

A glint came into the old man's eyes, and he led the way to a tumble-down garage in the corner of the driveway.

"Oh no, Da, come on. Fiona won't want to go in that old thing."

"She might," Fi said, glad of any excuse not to drive Mort's beast of a car.

The door ground open, banging on the ground as its hinge swung away from the doorframe. The old man swore in a stream of Cornish until he'd opened it wide enough that they could see inside. Fi frowned at the lumpy shape covered by a mouldy tarpaulin. He beamed at the two women then tugged the grey sheet.

Fi stared at the vintage van. There was a large dent in one side and so many chips in the navy-blue paintwork, it looked like a deliberate design choice.

"Getun," he said, his grin widening as he climbed into the cab.

Tamsyn rolled her eyes. "Sorry, it's his pride and joy. We can take your car, if you'd rather."

"Nope, I'm sure this is fine." Fi hopped up onto the front seat and Tamsyn joined her, slamming the passenger door shut. Anything to avoid driving.

Fi shifted on the lumpy seat. "Where's the seatbelt?"

The old man laughed and started the car. No seatbelts, then. Fi braced her hand on the dashboard as the van accelerated out of the garage.

Chapter 28

Fi's jaw chattered against her jaw as the van clattered along the drive. With a low growl, that might have been words, the old man turned onto the road. The van wobbled and Fi tensed, expecting it to topple over as he took the corner. She looked down at the sat nav on her phone and had to blink as she saw road speeding past under their feet. The blood drained from her face.

"There's a hole in the floor." Fi said it out loud as her mind processed what her eyes saw.

"Da's been working on this thing for years. He's done the engine, but the bodywork…well let's just say it needs some tender loving care."

"Nonsense, goes alreet, dunnee?" The old man patted the dashboard, and something banged inside the glove box.

Fi chose to ignore it. She was already in the van. "It's left up here."

A small blue fae appeared in the front pocket of his overalls. The piskie grinned as the van swerved around a corner. The old man laughed. It was a touch maniacal to Fi's ears, and she tensed again as the man veered the van down an unmarked road.

"Da says he knows a short cut."

Fi nodded, her jaw clenched tight as every bump in the road threw her up off the vinyl seat. She would never take suspension for granted again. The piskie bounced up and down, waving its arms like it was in a roller coaster. Fi stared straight ahead.

The old man said something then looked at her expectantly.

"He asked if you wanted to have a go."

"Oh, no thanks. I wouldn't know where to start."

Tamsyn's dad reached down and pulled a thermos from the car door. Why did he have tea in a car he kept hidden in a garage? Balancing it on his knees, he let go of the steering wheel and poured himself a cup of sludge coloured liquid. Fi grabbed the wheel, fighting to keep it straight as the van sped down the lane. A stream of curse words bubbled from her lips as the wheel battled, as if it wanted to swerve into the ditch by the side of the road.

"Wansum?" He offered her the flask. The tang of alcohol burned her nostrils. Not tea, then.

"No, thanks. Can I hold the mug for you, so you can drive?" Fi's voice had gone up an octave and wobbled in time with the van.

The old man laughed again and patted her hand before slurping down his drink and taking hold of the wheel once more. Back in control, he slammed the gear stick into third and revved the engine. Fi gave up on tracking their progress on sat nav and concentrated on gripping the seat and keeping her foot away from the hole in the floor.

When the van finally arrived at Mên-an-Tol, Fi staggered from the vehicle. She almost kissed the stubby grass that poked through the sandy dirt at the side of the road. Tamsyn's dad patted the van and pointed to a footpath across the field where a white tent flapped in the stiff breeze.

Piskies perched on every raised surface, lending a blue-ish tinge to the fence and trees. A trio clung to the top of the tent, their feet struggling for purchase on the canvas. Fi pulled her jacket tight and walked over to the police officer on duty.

"You can't go any further, miss. Police investigation."

"I know, I got an alert." Fi flashed her ID. "Piskies?"

The officer nodded, pulled back the tent flap and called for a detective. A harassed looking woman stepped outside. Tendrils of hair had escaped from her neat bun. She rubbed a hand over her eyes and looked down at Fi.

"Magical Liaison Office, huh? Make it quick. Coroner's on his way and it's ugly. The pests dragged him to the road after they…Who are they?" The officer glared at Tamsyn and her da over Fi's shoulder.

"Er, civilian consultants. Experts on the piskies," Fi lied, shuffling her feet, and praying her eyes didn't give her away.

"Do they know why the blighters killed a hitchhiker?"

"Our best guess is that he came too close to the piskie queen's home."

The detective narrowed her eyes. "This isn't a fairy tale. Someone is dead."

"I know. You and your officers should be careful. Don't wander over the fields. Stay by the road. And maybe offer them some food to show you don't mean any harm."

"Thanks for the advice." The officer rolled her eyes. "What are you planning to do?"

"We're going to look around, see if we can stop this happening again."

The detective's eyes softened, and she shook Fi's hand. "I hope you can. It's a mess in there."

Fi gulped. She didn't need to see the body to imagine what had happened.

"Do you want an escort?"

"No, thanks." The fewer people who got anywhere near the portal, the better.

Fi sucked in a breath, squared her shoulders, and strode past the tent, beckoning Tamsyn and her dad to follow.

Tamsyn's eyes widened as she saw the blood stains on the thick grass. She came up beside Fi. "Someone's been killed?" Her eyes darted left and right.

"Afraid so."

"Are we in danger?"

Fi opened her mouth to answer, but as they crossed into the field, the piskies fluttered into the sky from their perches, filling the air with chittering and gnashing teeth.

The small fae creatures clustered above the three people. Fi shrank back, drawing power to her hands. She glanced over her shoulder. The police had their guns out, aiming at the swarm in the sky. Not good.

The old man patted her on the shoulder and stepped in front. He reached into his pocket and brought out the injured piskie. He mumbled a few words and held it up in his palm, like an offering. The piskie stood and screeched a few words at its massing brethren.

A larger piskie swooped down and hovered in front of them. Its beetle-like eyes shone, reflecting the gathering clouds. It squeaked at the other piskie, and they had an animated conversation. Tamsyn's dad nodded along.

"S'reet," he chimed in.

"Any idea what they're saying?" Fi whispered out of the corner of her mouth.

"I think the piskie said that Austol helped it, and they shouldn't attack us."

"Who's Austol?"

"That's Da's name."

Fi nodded and shuffled her toes inside her shoes, her power still sparking over her skin. The larger piskie nodded and motioned to the rest, leading them back to their trees and fence. The police officers relaxed and put their guns away, keeping one hand over the holster, just in case. Fi didn't blame them. She kept her power close as she marched on towards the portal, the stares of thousands of tiny black eyes boring into her back.

Chapter 29

"So, what are we going to find?" Tamsyn darted forwards to keep up with Fi.

"That standing stone is a portal to the fae realm. I want to speak to this piskie queen and tell her to stop hurting the tourists."

"Bleddy emmets." The old man spat on the ground.

"What's an emmet?"

"It's the Cornish word for tourists. Da has…views on them."

"Sounds like they're the same views that Joan the Wad has. But if she doesn't stop, the government's going to wipe out all the piskies."

Austol let out a stream of curses. Well, Fi thought they were curses. She still couldn't understand his gravelly accent, but the tone was clear.

"Da likes the piskies, thinks they bring him luck, don't you, Da?"

In response, he patted the small creature in his hand and sang it a breathy lullaby. The piskie responded by biting him, but the old man just laughed and tickled it behind the ear. Fi made a face. How could he like an unlovable bug? But then, she had a grumpy dragon as a familiar…

As she studied the piskie lying on the man's palm, she noticed its little face turning this way and that and its pointed ears pricked up. It chattered and pushed back into the man's thumb. Fi cocked her head to one side and looked ahead. There was nothing there. Fi dismissed its weird behaviour and strode on.

Her foot sank into the ground. She cried out as she lost her balance and fell forward with a splat. Freezing water covered her and seeped between her clothes and into her shoes.

Fi spat out the dirt in her mouth and kicked her feet, trying to get some sort of purchase. Nothing. Panicking, she pushed on tufts of clumpy moss, each one sinking into the muck as soon as she applied any pressure. She changed tactic and did a few awkward swimming strokes, struggling to keep her head above the black brown water.

"Stay'un still."

"Keep still!" Tamsyn translated. Her voice sounded far away.

Fi twisted to see, but black sand got in her eye and earth filled her mouth as she choked on the thick dirt. Hands grabbed at her feet and her shoe sucked at her skin. More hands clawed at her waist and suddenly she was free.

She spat out black dirt and sucked in the clean air. Back on solid ground, she knelt, panting, fisting her hand into the spiky grass. She wiped her eyes free from the grit and breathed out a thank you to her rescuers.

Fi took a moment to steady her breathing before she pushed herself upright and glared at the piskie. She shivered as the breeze picked up, driving her sodden clothes against her skin. Fi abandoned her waterlogged jacket and hopped up and down. She studied the piskie. It turned its head slightly to the left. Fi picked up a small pebble from the ground and threw it ahead. It hit the ground with a ba-loop and then sank under thick, oozy mud. A quagmire. She selected another small stone and aimed it in the direction that the piskie stared.

The mermaid had said that piskies were related to will o'wisps and that Joan the Wad liked leading travellers astray. Perhaps, she'd spelled this whole area into an elaborate trap to stop people finding the portal to the fae realm. And the poor walker had blundered past her defences and ended up dead.

Fi narrowed her eyes and looked at the piskie again, bringing her head down so she was level with the small creature now settled in the breast pocket of Austol's dungarees. It blinked up at her with its huge black eyes and turned its head.

"That way. Slowly," she said between chattering teeth.

They made their way carefully across the field in a strange spiralling zig zag that made no sense. Fi saw a couple of police officers staring in their direction, muttering to themselves. She didn't blame them. Two women and an elderly man holding a piskie while they weaved across a field was a strange sight. Just when she thought they'd taken a wrong turn and were furthest from the standing stone, the piskie chattered and they made their way in an almost straight line to the circular stone.

Fi stopped a couple of metres away and stared it down. The stone was a little shorter than her, and about the same width. Other than the perfect round hole through the middle, it was an unimpressive grey colour that stuck out from the earthy tones of the surrounding field. Two other standing stones flanked it, reminding her of the digits 101 or a doughnut sandwich. She turned her mind away from error codes to the rest of the field. They had passed other large boulders on their winding route to this point, half buried and forgotten. Perhaps they had a purpose once, but no longer.

The piskie sat cross legged on Austol's hand, gazing at the portal. Fi narrowed her eyes and selected another stone from the ground. She threw it at the hole. It disappeared with a flash of purple light. They had found the portal to the fae realm.

Chapter 30

"Joan the Wad, Queen of the piskies, I am Fiona Blair of the Magical Liaison Office. I need to talk to you about the attacks."

Silence.

"Maybe you should curtsey, she's a queen after all."

Fi sucked her lip. It was worth a try, except she had no idea how to do that. She glanced at Tamsyn who was in a perfect ballerina curtsey and copied her, wobbling as her body bent into the unfamiliar shape.

Long seconds of silence stretched over the field. The dark clouds above rumbled with the promise of a spring storm. Fi shivered as the wind picked up, whipping her hair around her face and into her eyes and pressing her soaking clothes against her skin. Fat drops of rain splattered onto the ground and Fi blinked to clear her vision. The portal shimmered.

A piskie twice the size of the one Austol carried stepped through the stone. It held a sharp spear.

It spoke some words and Austol repeated them more slowly. Fi looked between them, unable to understand the language. Tamsyn picked up the translation.

"He says the queen has deigned to grant us an audience. We may enter."

"You don't have to come with me. It could be dangerous. Thanks for getting me this far."

"Nonsense. We're not passing up the chance to see a piskie queen." Tamsyn nodded to her dad. "This is practically heritage."

Austol took a step towards the portal. Fi laid a hand on his arm. "I'm serious. I don't know what's in there. I'll do my best to protect you, but…I might not be strong enough."

He spoke in a low tone, his eyes so full of kindness and trust that Fi thought her heart would burst, even if she couldn't understand the words. He patted her hand, nodded to the large piskie and strolled through the portal, vanishing in a flash of violet light. Tamsyn bobbed her head at Fi and followed him through, swallowed by a swirl of the same bright light.

Fi sucked in a breath and followed after. The ground lurched beneath her feet, and she swayed as she struggled to stay upright, fighting the strange sensation of portal travel. It was the same disorientation she had felt when she'd tried a VR headset for the first time, but magnified by a hundred. Once her head stopped spinning, the first thing she noticed was the sky. It was pink. But the strangest thing were the green shimmers that floated across the pinkish sky, like northern lights only larger and coming in wave after wave of magic.

A murmur drew her attention from the enchanting sky, and she jerked to attention as she noticed the rows of piskies standing among the long grass, watching them.

Unlike the palm sized versions that flitted around outside, these piskies had more variety. Their skin ranged in shade from a midnight blue so dark it was almost black to a pale duck egg blue, and they were all larger than the piskies outside – the tallest came up to Fi's knee – but they had the same dark eyes bulging from their faces.

A small piskie tugged at a larger one's brown dress and pointed before someone hushed it. A child. There were piskie children. Fi didn't know why that surprised her. One stared at her with large eyes and a lopsided grin that reminded Fi of her niece back home. Fi smiled back and the child piskie waved shyly before its parent picked it up.

"The queen will see you now." Pointy Stick gestured past the gathered piskies to a small tunnel carved in the moss-covered mound that bubbled up in front of them. It reminded Fi of the barrows that she'd seen on school trips in fields back in the Cotswolds. She'd always thought they were graves of long-dead warriors, not royal fae courts.

Tamsyn and her dad ducked through, and Fi swallowed hard before she followed after, bending so she didn't scrape her head on the granite tunnel. Dusky fae lights glowed in the rock, providing a dim lustre in the tunnel that meant they could see. Low doorways on either side of the passage led into dark rooms, more than seemed possible from the mound above ground.

Fi caught glimpses of piskies sleeping, their pointed faces relaxed and wings still, and others tearing the flesh from a dead animal, barely chewing it with their sharp teeth before they swallowed it down. In another room, tiny children piskies skipped and played a game with sticks in a creche, one large teacher piskie sat on a stool and read a story in that language they had that sounded like it was all consonants.

There was an entire society down here. What would happen if the government decided to wipe out the piskies? Would it stop at the pests who lived in the human world or would they go further and exterminate all these fae? Fi's thoughts spiralled as they walked. And would it stop there or were there fae alliances? If mundanes attacked the piskies, which other fae courts might retaliate?

She winced. Deep in her thoughts, she had straightened her neck and jarred her head on the roof of the passage. Pointy Stick snickered at her pain and motioned for her to keep walking. How long did this stupid tunnel go on for? Fi rubbed her head and bent over further to make sure she didn't scrape against the roof again.

The pressure of the enclosed corridor lifted and the three people stumbled into a huge chamber. Fi blinked as the wattage increased from the dull, barely there light of the tunnel to a roaring blaze that resembled daylight. If daylight flicked between bright pink, violet and turquoise.

Once her eyes had adjusted, she gaped. The room stretched up, almost as high as a cathedral, which defied any natural laws of science because she was sure the passageway hadn't sloped down enough for the dimensions to fit under the mound. Must be fae magic at work.

Here the piskies wore silky furs and gauzy material that left little to the imagination. Two guards flanked a huge throne made of rose-coloured crystal, their sharp flint spearheads glinting in the pink light. Atop the throne sat the largest piskie Fi had seen.

She wore flimsy clothes that looked like they'd been woven from mist, for all that they barely covered her plump body. Her skin, that Fi could see far too much of, was a bright blue that reminded Fi of the screen of death she had seen so many times as an IT consultant and a crown of bones sat on her head, woven into her violent pink hair that clashed with her skin. The crown was topped with a pair of pointed antlers that added another half a foot in height to the squat queen. Her clawed hands cradled a polished stick with a quartz that matched the colour of the throne tied to the top. This must be the piskie queen.

Beside the queen, a tall piskie – a hair smaller than the queen – glowered at them and bared his pointed teeth, while on her other side, a grey-haired piskie watched them with interest.

Tamsyn sank into a curtsey and Austol bowed. Fi dipped a small bow, keeping her eyes on the oversized piskie. The queen said something, her voice surprisingly light in the quiet cavern. Fi looked to Austol to translate, then to Tamsyn as he garbled out something in an accent too thick for her to understand.

"She said 'Welcome to our throne room, strangers. What purpose have you at the piskie court?' "

155

Chapter 31

Fi stepped forward and met the queen's glittering black eyes. Joan the Wad raised a hand and Fi felt a sickly-sweet sensation rush through her as if she'd eaten too much sugar. She shuddered and opened her mouth to complain when she noticed her arm. It was free from the muck of the bog, and she was dry.

"Thank you," she said, still staring at her clean clothes.

"Consider it a boon from the Queen of Cornwall. We cannot have a filthy beast in our presence. Now, state your purpose," the queen said though the translators.

Fi screwed up her face, unsure who this 'we' was before she realised that the queen was referring to herself. She coughed. "I am Fiona Blair, an agent of the Magical Liaison Office and I ask you to stop the attacks on tourists."

Joan's eyes narrowed. "The 'tourists', as you call them, are invaders. They are an unwelcome blight on our land. Our minions merely chase them out."

"Your piskies have killed at least two people and injured many more. My boyfriend is at home with a head injury because of your attacks. And your people are injured in them too." She pointed to the small piskie sitting on Austol's hand.

"Ah yes, our brave soldiers. Unfortunate casualties of a necessary war, but they live to serve their queen, do you not, little one?"

The piskie made a clicking noise and lowered its head.

"We have tried to live in peace with the humans, but you expand like a rash to cover every part of the land. You destroy our sacred sites with tarmac and housing, and you speak to us about 'right'." The queen scoffed and shifted on her chair, exposing even more of herself before the misty clothes fell into new folds around her blue body. "Right would be if you all left and let us live in peace."

"Why not live in peace here, in your realm?"

Joan screwed up her face. "Although we may be more powerful than useless mortals, we are not welcome in the honourless fae courts, and they have conspired to keep us in this small, unworthy corner of the fae realm unable to expand and grow as we may wish. So, we must seek new lands for our people. This Cornwall may not be perfect, but the smaller members of our court scavenge a life there, and we were respected there, once. The name Joan the Wad used to mean something in the lands of Cornwall."

"So, you want land. Let me talk to the government about granting you some. Just stop the attacks—"

"We think not."

"Then why did you grant us an audience?"

"This man," Austol bowed his head again as Joan acknowledged him, "This kind, sweet man – cared for one of our people when the rest of you kill us without a care. For him, we said we would listen. And we have heard your request. And our answer is no."

"Your majesty, perhaps we should listen to this witch." A grey-haired piskie stepped forward, his head bowed. "She is not a mundane, and she was sent by the people in power. The humans have taken your threat seriously. Perhaps we can reason with them."

He gave Fi a pleading look and she picked up his thread. "Oh yes. The government is debating this in parliament. You've been recognised for sure. So can we – you – call off your piskies and we can negotiate?"

The queen ignored Fi and shook her head at the grey-haired piskie. "Balwr, we have discussed this before. You have too much sympathy for the humans. Our answer is no."

"But–" Fi couldn't help it, she had to try.

"You dare to question the Queen's will?" The tall piskie stepped forward, a wicked spear in his clawed hands.

Fi put her hands up. "I–"

"You dare to tell us how to manage our court?" Joan the Wad stood and glared down at Fi from her raised dais.

"No, I just–"

"You think you can come here and tell us that after centuries of harm by humans, we should leave them alone and accept a token from your rulers, if they even bother to reply to you, agent of the Magical Liaison Office. No. This will not stand."

"You have to listen." Fi ignored the grey-haired piskie as he gestured for her to stop. She had to make them listen. "They will kill you, all of you. You'll harm your people if you don't back off."

Joan's hands clenched around her sceptre. The crystal at the top flickered like fire. "Not if we kill them first. Prepare everyone to attack."

"My queen," a small voice spoke from a dark corner.

"You!" Joan whirled around and pointed her staff at the speaker, illuminating the woman. Fi gasped to see the shopkeeper who had sold her ointment for Cressida's scale rot in the piskie realm. Her head reeled. Demelza was in league with the piskies all along. Fi narrowed her eyes at the piskie 'expert', spy, more like.

The woman bowed low. "My queen," she started again.

"Demelza of Zennor, you have failed us. We tasked you to keep our realm safe from intruders and here are three who have made it past your wards and our illusions."

Demelza held up her hands. "No! I came to warn you about her. That they are trying to stop you."

"So you admit you know this witch!" Demelza sputtered at Joan's accusation. "Silence traitor!"

Demelza fell to her knees. "Your majesty, I am sorry. I will make amends but killing people...you never said people would die. It's not right."

"We do not ask for your opinions. We granted you luck and prosperity for your insignificant shop and you tell people how to get into our realm."

"No, I never–"

"Silence!"

Demelza cowered away from the queen.

"You shall pay in amusement for our court. Dance." The piskie queen aimed her crystal sceptre at Demelza and a blast of pink magic shot at her feet. The shopkeeper shrieked and jumped to one side as the piskies hooted with laughter.

Demelza wasn't quick enough to dodge the next bolt of magic and she sank to the ground with a cry of pain.

"Enough dancing?" Joan mocked, aiming for Demelza again.

"Wait! Please," Fi darted forwards, shielding the shopkeeper with her body.

"You have spirit, white-haired witch, but she betrayed us."

"There must be something we can do…"

Joan the Wad stood and glided over to Fi, her wings fluttering, keeping her at eye level with the witch. "Perhaps this witch cares so passionately for the invaders that she is willing to play a game."

An excited chattering rumbled around the cavern in a wave of sound. Fi swallowed.

"What sort of game?"

"We will set you a challenge. If you win, we will leave the invaders alone."

"And if I lose?"

"Then we continue to protect our lands, and you forfeit your life to serve us."

Nerrissa's warning rang through Fi's mind. Don't bargain with the fae. Don't trust the piskie queen. But she had no choice. This was a chance to stop the death and save the species, even if the queen didn't want them saved. There were piskie families here and it wasn't their fault she controlled them. It wasn't right that they could be wiped out because of her stupidity.

Fi swallowed. "You have to promise to let Tamsyn and Austol go."

"We would never harm a follower of the old ways. They are free to go as they please."

"And Demelza, she should face human justice for whatever crimes she committed."

Joan frowned and tapped her sceptre against her hand. "Fine. What is the life of a human to us? We are generous and will spare her too."

"Then I'll do it."

A slow smile spread over the queen's bright face and her eyes glittered. She raised her sceptre and her voice reverberated around the room, amplified by magic. "You heard her. The witch has agreed to a match of champions."

"Wait, what?"

Chapter 32

A roar went up around the huge cavern as the piskies cheered, clapping their hands, and flapping their wings in excitement.

"Hang on, what is a match of champions?"

The grey-haired piskie – Balwr, the queen had called him – sidled up to Fi. "It's a fight. You have to defeat the queen's champion."

"A fight? I never agreed to a fight." Fi looked around for support but found only the glittering eyes of piskies eager for blood.

Balwr leaned in. "You agreed to the match. If you bow out now, she will kill you."

Fi stared down at him. His face was sympathetic. He wasn't joking. Fi's breath came faster. She never wanted to fight. Under her skin, what remained of her magic prickled at her whirling emotions. She couldn't do it. She wouldn't.

Her eyes lit on a piskie child sucking its thumb. The child was dressed in leaves and had a stick toy carved into some beast with large eyes and horns; the piskie equivalent of a teddy bear, perhaps.

If she didn't fight, all of these piskies would be exterminated. Not to mention the human casualties when they invaded Cornwall. And would they stop at the border with Devon? Or would they carry on further north? Maybe even to the Cotswolds where her family lived.

Her niece's face flashed through her mind and Fi clenched her fists. She could prevent a war. She would prevent a war.

"OK, right." It should be simple enough. Fi cricked her neck and jumped up and down on her feet to warm up. Even the large queen only came up to her thigh, she'd just fall on whichever piskie was unlucky enough to fight her and pin it down to the count of three.

"You don't understand–"

With a wave of the sceptre, the underground cavern melted away, replaced by an arena covered with sand. It reminded Fi of a gladiator circus from Roman times, except the seats floated in tiers above the arena and piskies zoomed around between them, chattering and glancing down at her.

The queen had her own box, a platform covered with crystals that shimmered in the artificial fae light. Pointy Stick and a few other members of her court flanked her, reclining on mossy couches and stuffing oozing purple berries into their wide mouths.

Demelza disappeared from where she cowered on the floor and reappeared between two guards at Joan's feet in her royal box. She peeked over the edge and shouted something to Fi. It was lost in the noise of thousands of excited piskies.

The sympathetic piskie shook his head. "I am sorry." He flew up to join the queen in her box.

"Fiona Blair, of the Magical Liaison Office, has agreed to fight my champion in a fight to the death."

Death. The word rang round Fi's head. This wasn't what she'd agreed to. The blood drained from her face and her hands felt numb. The mermaid was right, she shouldn't have entered into the stupid bargain, but what other choice did she have? How else could she stop the attacks if the stupid queen wouldn't listen?

"If she wins, we have promised to release her and the traitor Demelza and stop attacking the invaders who intrude upon our lands."

A chorus of boos went around the arena and the piskies pelted berries at Fi.

"Ouch!" Fi glared and clenched her fists. The remainder of her magic swirled under her skin, but she kept it clamped down. She didn't have much left after Land's End, and she had to save it for the fight.

"If she loses, her life is forfeit."

"Wait," Fi shouted, noticing that the two humans still stood next to her, frozen to their spots as they gaped around the arena. "You promised that Tamsyn and Austol could go."

What was she thinking bringing innocent humans to this death trap? Stupid, stupid, stupid.

"I did. They are free to go…except…" Joan's grin broadened. "They have been good friends to the piskies…champions even…"

"What?"

"Would you be our champion, Austol of Cornwall and friend of piskies?"

Chapter 33

The old man swallowed, and his weathered face faded from a tanned brown to a jaundiced yellow. His eyes darted around the arena.

Fi folded her arms. "This wasn't the agreement."

Joan narrowed her eyes. "You agreed to fight our champion. We have chosen our champion. Now you will fight."

"You can't choose Da, he's an old man." Tamsyn stepped in front of her father. "I'll be your champion."

"How touching. Now we have two champions. Well, witch," Joan spat the word, "who will you fight?"

Fiona's mind raced and her gaze lit on the tunnel. It was her fault these innocent humans were here, and she needed to protect them. Joan leaned forward on her seat and crammed a fistful of purple berries into her wide mouth. Dark juice ran down her pointed chin. She wanted entertainment. Well, Fi wouldn't give it to her.

The witch strode over to Tamsyn and Austol.

"What do we do?" Tamsyn wrung her hands together, sweat beading on her forehead.

"Lie down."

"What?"

"Joan wants a fight. We're not going to give it to her. Lie down. I'll distract her and you run."

Tamsyn and Austol exchanged a glance then the old man shrugged and lowered himself to the ground.

"What are you doing?" screeched Joan.

"Looks like your champions concede to me. I win." Fi folded her arms and walked towards the box, keeping the queen's gaze on her.

"No."

"Those were your terms."

"Our terms were to death. Our champions are still living." Joan licked her lips.

"Not much of a fight though, was it? If that's the best you can do…" Fi swallowed down the fear that pulsed through her. Goading the queen wasn't a smart move but it was all she had to protect Austol and Tamsyn who had trusted her. She shrugged and turned away from the queen, catching Tamsyn's eye and mouthing at her to run. "Looks like the piskies won't have a chance, even if you do invade Cornwall if this is your best."

She span round and shrugged at the queen. Out of the corner of her eye, Fi saw Tamsyn help Austol to his feet and they scrambled to the tunnel that would lead to the portal.

"No!" Joan pointed with her staff and piskies streamed out of their seats towards the humans.

"Where is your honour?" Fi shouted, waving her arms to get Joan's attention. "This man and his daughter are friends to your people, and you don't have many of them outside in the mortal realm, and you want to reward their friendship by killing them?" Fi shook her head. "Shame on you, Queen Joan the Wad, and shame on your people. No wonder you were banished from the rest of the fae realm if this is your idea of honour."

"We are honourable!" Joan jumped to her feet. "How dare you speak to me of honour, witch!"

Looks like she'd hit a nerve. Fi pressed on, "Then let them go."

Joan tilted her head to one side. "You have a bargain in mind, witch."

"Let them go and send me a real champion." Fi lifted one shoulder and turned away from the queen. "Or acknowledge defeat."

Joan considered it for a long minute before nodding her head. Her guards released Tamsyn and Austol, who stood trembling in the arena.

"Go on, get out of here," Fi hissed.

"We should stay to support you. What if you get into trouble?" asked Tamsyn, still shaking with fear.

Too late. Fi was already in trouble up to her neck, and though her heart swelled at the human offering to help her, she couldn't let them stay and risk their lives. Not again. "I can't concentrate if you're here. Please, I have to know you're safe. Wait for me outside the portal. If I'm not out in a couple of hours, call the Magical Liaison Office and ask for Agent Jones. Tell her everything. She'll know what to do."

"But–"

"Please," Fi begged. She couldn't lose them, and if they stayed, Joan might have a change of heart and kill them anyway.

Tamsyn nodded and led her dad away to the tunnel that would take them to the portal.

Fi stared straight ahead at the queen. She wouldn't be able to understand Joan now, but that probably didn't matter. She knew what she had to do. Fight a piskie champion. She bobbed up and down on her feet. If only she'd taken Cressida's snipes about her lack of fitness seriously. Too late to regret not doing more exercise now.

Cheers sounded and Joan grinned down at Fi, her sharp teeth glinting in the fae light. "Bring in my champion."

A stone gate rattled up from thin air, appearing on the other side of the arena to the tunnel, and the crowd went silent, thousands of black eyes stared at the gate as it swung up.

"Let the game begin!"

Chapter 34

Fi looked around. She could understand the queen. How was that possible? She caught the eye of the grey-haired piskie, and he winked at her just as she registered the candyfloss taste on her tongue. Fae magic. She turned her attention back to Joan. The queen had an evil glint in her black, bug-like eyes. That couldn't be good.

The gate opened fully. Fi squinted at the gloom. A rumbling roar sounded from deep within the murky darkness. *What was in there?*

A humongous, webbed foot poked out through the gate, followed by another and then the creature sat on the sand. Fi stared up at it. A toad. A giant toad, but still…this was the champion?

The beast sat just outside the gate and licked its yellow eyeball with a long pink tongue. A flash of movement caught its attention up in the stands and its tongue shot out, grabbing a piskie. It pulled the struggling fae to its wide mouth and chomped down. The piskie's screams were drowned out by the slobbery chomping of the ginormous amphibian. The queen laughed.

Fi backed away. *Don't get caught by the tongue.* That mantra ran through her head as she edged back, away from the creature. Maybe it would get bored and head back into its cave. Two guards in armour made from tree bark prodded the toad in the rear. It shuffled forward, then turned and struck out with its tongue.

With a wet slap, the tongue slammed into the stone gate as it banged shut, the guards' chests heaving as they eyed the creature. OK, so it's not going back in the cave. But all she had to do was stay out of its way, maybe it would get full of eating piskies from the audience and go to sleep. It was almost like a reptile, right? And her familiar definitely slept after she ate.

The toad turned its head, surveying the room. Its yellow eyes landed on Fi, crouching on the sand, trying to make herself look as small and unappetising as possible. It let out a loud croak and tensed its body. Its muscles quivered, then it leapt across the arena, landing next to Fi.

Fi screamed and scrambled backwards, away from the fae beast. So it could clear the cavernous arena with one bound. Fantastic.

The toad shuffled round and took a step forward. Fi dived to the side and its webbed foot landed on the sand where she had stood a split second before. This thing could crush her with one step. This wasn't a fair fight.

She moved behind the toad, holding her breath in case it could hear her. Fi's eyes searched the room. She needed a weapon. Edging away, her back pressed against a solid wall. So the open arena was an illusion. The stone walls were still there. A brown stick lay stark on the white sand. A spear. One of the guards had dropped it. That would have to do. She crept along the wall.

The toad hadn't noticed her behind it yet. Its moist skin glistened with an unhealthy pink sheen in the bright fae lights that hovered above them. It pushed backwards, settling into a seated position. Fi gulped as its wet skin pressed against her. The stench of rotten earth and mouldy water threatened to choke her. The amphibian didn't notice her. Fi slid along the wall as fast as she could, the pressure increasing as the toad leaned into the rock and rearranged its feet to get comfortable in its sitting position.

Her chest burned as it crushed her against the wall. Only its slippery skin allowed her to keep moving. Fi's hands clutched at the wall, getting whatever purchase she could to move forwards. With an unimpressive slushing sound, her torso broke free from behind the creature. She sucked in a deep breath, her head spinning as oxygen flooded her lungs. She forced one leg free, then the other, amazed that the toad was still oblivious to nearly killing her.

Fi hugged the wall and moved to the spear. Nearly there. Come on. The toad studied the piskies with its bulbous yellow eyes. She could do this. A piskie floating on a seat above her shouted and pointed down, drawing the toad's attention to where she stood. Fi glared at the piskie. *Not fair.* The toad scooted round, and its eyes rested on the white-haired witch.

Its muscles bunched, and it launched itself across the arena.

173

Fi dived for the spear and scooped it up, her feet slipping in the sand as she forced her legs to move. In her hands, it was less a spear and more a large stick, but it was a weapon and holding it gave her comfort. The toad landed with two of its webbed feet on the wall. It stared at them, testing its pads. Maybe it didn't realise the arena had walls. How smart were toads?

Fi didn't have much time to think about the comparative intelligence of toads compared to any other creature because the amphibian shot out its tongue and gripped Fi by the waist. The witch clawed at the wet, sticky pink pad pressed against her waist. It didn't move. Drool dripped down her front. *Disgusting.* Ugh, now she sounded like Cressida. Fi dug her heels into the sand and leaned back, fighting against the pull towards its gaping maw.

It drew her closer, unbothered by her wriggling. Fi tensed as she felt its hot breath wash over her body. With a cry, she plunged the sharpened spear into its flesh. Red blood spurted from the wound and the toad gave a strangled croak. Above her, a cheer went up at the sight of blood. Its grip around her loosened and Fi staggered away, ripping the spear out of its tongue.

She wiped her shaking hands on her top, leaving a smear of blood and toad saliva over the printed videogame logo. Fi backed away, spear held out as if she knew what she was doing.

The queen clapped slowly. "Bravo, well played. This will be more interesting than we hoped."

Not if Fi could help it. The toad rubbed at its mouth with its front foot, shaking its head from side to side. It croaked again. There was a note of anger in its deep voice. Fi stared. Could toads have emotions? She glanced up at Joan, who regarded the creature with a strange intensity. Maybe they had some sort of bond…if it was anything like the bond she had with Cressida, Joan could feed it power and emotion. But, she also felt when Cressida was hurt.

Joan stood and her sceptre shone as her sickly magic built. "We don't want to make it too easy for our champion, do we?"

The toad shuddered then split into three enormous beasts across the arena. Fi's mouth dropped open.

"Excellent illusion, my queen," said the grey-haired advisor, loud enough so Fi could hear.

Fi shot a look of thanks to the older piskie who seemed to be on her side. Of course, it was a trick. Joan the Wad was queen of illusions and tricks.

The three huge toads turned their yellow eyes on her, long tongues lolling from the side of their mouths and bloody saliva trickling down their swamp-green skin. They all looked so real. Fi kept her eyes on the one in the middle. That was the real one.

The queen stood and snapped her blue fingers. The arena spun round Fi in a blur, the toads merging into one green blob. She fell to the ground, the sand shifting beneath her feet. She dug her hands into the cool grains of sand, grounding herself. Above her, the piskies whirled round in a streak of blue and grey.

As quickly as it had started, the arena stopped. Fi lurched to the side, face planting into the sand. She pushed herself up, swaying from side to side as her body fought the dizziness. This was a million times worse than portal travel. When she looked up, nine toads stared back at her. Nine? She blinked. The nine images coalesced and blurred together until they became three. Her eyes focused on the trio of toads.

They were in the same positions as before, maybe they were as dizzy as she was. The beast in the middle launched itself into the air, unaffected by the spinning arena. Fi staggered to the side as it crashed into the sand beside her. It shifted on its feet. It looked real.

Fi threw her spear. Her PE teacher would have been proud – and astonished – if he'd been there to see her perfect javelin form. The spear arced through the air and into the toad's slitted nostril. It passed through and stuck in the sand. An illusion.

Fi walked through it and grabbed her spear. The sticky sweet sensation of fae magic bubbled over her skin and the illusion disappeared as soon as she touched it. Good to know. But she didn't want to get close enough to the real toad by mistake. She weighed the spear and eyed the other two toads. What now?

She still had some magic, not much, but it might be enough to injure it. Fi tested her power, pulling it to the surface for a moment and felt more than she expected. She concentrated and felt the hum of electricity in the crowd. Technically, she could pull on the electricity that powered living things, but she refused to cause more deaths than she had to. Fi pushed her magic to one side, focusing on the two giant creatures that blinked in unison on the opposite side of the arena. Best not to risk it in case she siphoned the life force from innocent piskies.

Backing away, putting as much distance between herself and the fae creatures as she could, she hit the invisible wall again. How could she make a plan if she couldn't even see the edge of the arena? An idea crept into her head.

The toad wasn't fast, but it put all its energy into jumping. If she could get it to leap full speed into the wall, that could knock it out. Just like when a kart smashed into a wall in the videogames she aced. But, she needed to know which of the two remaining toads was real.

She ran forward, jumping and shouting, drawing them in. The toads looked at her, their mouths drooped open. In tandem, they bunched their muscles and leapt at her. She launched into a baseball style slide and skidded between them, the sand scraping over her grazed skin. Fi gritted her teeth and rolled to her feet.

She eyed the arena, trying to gauge the distance to the wall.

"Come on then!" she yelled and ran to where she hoped a wall would be.

The gigantic animals croaked and leapt again. They collided in mid-air, the final illusion vanishing in a pop of violet light. The remaining toad didn't even blink. Was it used to fighting with Joan's illusion magic? It soared over Fi's head, aiming to land in front of her and cut off her escape.

The trajectory of its leap took it directly into the royal box. Joan flicked her fingers and the seats darted out of the way, parting before the huge amphibian. Piskies shouted and dropped whatever they held onto the arena floor as they grasped their flying seats in panic.

Demelza cried as she was shaken from the royal box. Her fingers reached for one of the rails, but the box lurched to the left, and she fell to the ground with a crunch.

Fi dived to the side and scrambled away in the sand. Everything relied on her judgement. She tensed, ready to run again. Then the toad hit the side of the arena headfirst. It flipped up so its warty back splattered on the wall before it sank headfirst to the sand.

"There," Fi shouted up at Joan, who stood, clutching the rail of her royal box. "I've beaten your champion."

The queen's lips pursed. Then she smiled. "We believe we said, 'to the death'. Our champion is not dead."

Fi's mouth dropped open. "You don't seriously want me to kill it. It's unconscious."

Joan cocked her head to one side. "You seem to misunderstand our agreement. But, if you are so concerned for him, then we shall heal him."

"What? No, that's not fair."

A shimmer of purple light rippled from the sceptre and coated the toad like a second skin. Fi stepped back at the force of the sticky fae magic and gagged at the sudden sweet taste in her mouth. With her power so depleted, she could sense other magic more vividly and the sugary coating on her tongue was worse than downing a can of energy drink.

"But, we are generous and let it not be said that the Queen of the piskies is without honour…perhaps the witch needs help. The traitor can fight at your side."

Demelza gaped in horror and clutched at Fi's arm. "No, no, no, no."

Fi ignored her and kept her eyes on the toad as it shook out its feet and rose up again.

Chapter 36

Fi backed away from the recovering toad, dragging Demelza with her. An earthy sensation brushed her skin at the contact, making Fi feel like her arm was coated in mud. She ignored it. Above them, piskies snickered and pointed. Great.

"Can you run?"

"My ankle!" Demelza gestured to the swollen foot that the queen had blasted.

That was a no, then. Fi kept her eyes on the beast. "Any ideas?"

"Maybe you can get it to crash into the wall again…"

They eyed the beast. Its muscles tensed, but then it shook its head, sending a gobbet of bloody saliva flying onto sand. Instead, it lurched forward in a crouching hop.

"Looks like it's learned its lesson…" Or the queen was telling it what to do through their bond. Fi eyed Joan. Her pointed face was screwed up in concentration and her black eyes stared unblinking at the toad. Fantastic. So, they were up against a toad controlled by a spiteful piskie.

"What do we do?" Demelza's voice spiked up in panic. "We've got to get out of here. Got to warn everyone."

"Tamsyn's doing that." Fi shook the shopkeeper's shoulders, watching the toad out of the corner of her eye. This was no time for hysterics. That was a lie. It was a perfect time to panic, it just wouldn't help.

"She said it was just to get some land back, but – my goddess, what was I thinking? I've caused this. I trusted her. I placed the stones, I helped with the wards–"

Fi slapped Demelza. Hard. This was no time for a breakdown or insane rambling. "Pull it together. This isn't your fault. It's her." She jerked her head to where Queen Joan sat in the royal box. Fi prayed that Demelza would believe her lie. A lot of the trouble in Cornwall had been caused by Demelza placing those dratted stones, but there wasn't time to get into nuances if they wanted to get out alive.

"I'll distract it, you stay close to the edge. If you can, get a weapon and sneak up behind it. We just need to finish this, and everything will work out OK." Fi managed to put some conviction in her voice, like she believed it.

Demelza nodded, her eyes large and full of trust. It was too much. Fi felt like a fraud, but she had to try, or else they were all doomed.

Fi sprinted off, waving her spear. She almost tripped over something on the sand. A phone. What was that doing in the fae realm?

A loud crunch told her the toad was behind her. She ignored the phone and kept running. She glanced over her shoulder, hoping Demelza had found a weapon. Fi skidded to a halt.

The toad towered over the shopkeeper. Up in her box, a wicked grin spread across Joan's face. She was going to kill Demelza. Fi knew it as surely as she knew how to clear the cache on her computer's memory. She swore.

With a grunt, Demelza flung up her arm and rocks grew from the ground in front of her, forming a cave. Fi gaped. So, Demelza had magic. The toad placed one giant webbed foot on the stone and scaled it. The rocks shifted. Demelza's cave wouldn't last for long under the weight of the creature.

On instinct, Fi reached for the remainder of her power. And the phone in the sand buzzed. Fi stared at it and the idea grew. If the fae had electricity, she would take it and use it. She hated what her power could do, that it lent itself to destruction. But this was life or death. She could use her magic to save Demelza and the tourists Joan wanted to kill, and the piskies the queen would destroy if she continued down this path.

And all it would cost was the life of a toad. And another shred of her humanity. More nightmares. More self-hate for killing a living being, yet again.

Demelza shrieked. A child screamed from somewhere up above and buried its head against its parent's chest.

Fi's humanity was a small price to pay to save so much. Fi gathered all the power she could find in the room to her, feeling her hair prickle up as electricity flowed into her from phones and whatever other devices the piskies had here.

"Hey!" she shouted.

The toad and queen turned in unison to stare at her.

"What happens when a toad gets hit by lightning?" Fi quipped, saying the first thing that came into her head. Not exactly lightning, but the results were the same. She blasted it with a bolt of electricity, draining every single mobile phone in the audience and shorting any electrical item she could find with the sudden burst of power.

The toad shivered, its green skin turning red where Fi hit it. It twitched and its feet splayed out from its body. Fi emptied every ounce of magic into it until she could feel its own electrical pulse, the same one that every living being had, fade away. She cut off her magic, the barest trickle left swirling deep within her.

It didn't explode. It wasn't like in the X-men movie. It just lay there, red streaks marking its skin with spidery threads, its eyes wide and staring. Fi finished the quote anyway, hating herself even as she forced her back straight. "The same thing that happens to everything else."

There was complete silence over the arena. Fi felt the thousands of glittering eyes on her and she kept her head high as she walked stiffly over to Demelza's cave, panting hard at the sudden exertion, and knocked on the stone. "It's over now."

Demelza peeped out and let the stones fall to one side. She stared at the dead toad. "Thank you," she whispered.

Fi nodded and turned to the queen.

"There," Fi spat, "I've done it. Now back off and leave the tourists free."

Joan the Wad smiled down at her, sharp teeth glinting in the fae lights. "No."

Chapter 37

"You promised." Fae couldn't lie, could they? And they had to keep to their vows…Fi was sure she had read that somewhere.

"I promised I would release you and Demelza and stop the attacks."

Fi screwed up her face. What was she missing?

"But, I didn't say when." Joan wagged her long index finger and her voice had a sing-song quality to it as she beamed down from her royal box.

Fi swore. Tricky fae. "What about your honour?"

A murmur went round the crowd. They weren't all happy with their queen's decision. The grey-haired piskie frowned and she heard a male voice in her head. *Run.*

She didn't need to be told twice. Fi grabbed Demelza and tugged her towards the exit.

"No!" Joan shouted. Fi heard snaps as the piskies unfurled their wings and then the swoosh of a horde of piskies taking flight.

She dragged Demelza along. They were nearly at the tunnel. They could make it. They were at the entrance. So close.

Demelza staggered to one side. "Go! I'll catch up. I'll seal the tunnel."

Fi stared, as Demelza sank to the ground and with a desperate snap of power, the shopkeeper tugged on the corridor walls with her magic. The tunnel shook and Fi stumbled into the wall.

"Run!" Demelza shouted over her shoulder. "I'll follow."

Fi scrambled backwards. She dodged lumps of falling granite, coughing as dust clawed its way into her mouth and lungs. She sprinted, escaping the rockslide. The strange light of the fae sky shimmered at the end of the tunnel. Nearly there. She pressed herself against the cool wall to avoid another rock fall and dived forwards. After fifteen more paces, she realised there were no more rocks crashing around her. She was clear. She turned back. The tunnel was completely blocked.

"Demelza!" Fi forced the shout from her dry mouth before she collapsed in a fit of coughing. The rocks stayed stubbornly still. Fi crawled forwards and prised a small piece of granite free with shaking hands. It revealed more rocks. Demelza had sacrificed herself. Fi's chest heaved. Why?

She leant against the smooth wall of the corridor and pressed her hands into her eyes. What could she have done differently? Was there a way she could have saved Demelza? A small sob racked her body. And now she was crying.

The woman might have placed the stones for Joan, but she should have lived to face justice rather than die under a pile of rubble.

She heard Tamsyn's voice calling her name from far away. In a daze, she headed for the light at the end of the tunnel, tripping over her own feet as she moved towards freedom.

A scrape behind her made Fi's head snap round. Demelza had made it. She hurried back to help, clawing at the large rocks.

"Demelza, I'm here."

A chunk of granite shifted and fell to the ground. Fi moved to the small hole, then shrank back. A blue hand reached through, scrabbling at the remaining rubble. Piskies.

The shrieks of unnumbered fae creatures filled the tunnel, deafening the witch. Fi stumbled backwards then fled, not waiting to see if they had breached the rockfall.

Chapter 38

Fi sprinted across the small meadow of long grass and strange flowers to the circular stone that marked the barrier between the fae and mortal realms. She looked over her shoulder in time to see blue bodies in the dim light of the tunnel. Fi dived through the portal, closing her eyes as the wave of nausea hit her. She landed in a heap on wet, spiky grass.

She blinked up, eyes squinted against the torrential rain. Soft hands lifted her upright. Tamsyn. Fi shook her head.

"Fi? Are you alright?"

No. No she wasn't alright. She had killed with her magic. Again. Demelza had died to save her. The entirety of Joan's court was seconds away from crossing into the human realm, intent on killing her and possibly every human in Cornwall. Fi felt sick.

What could she do? She reached for her magic, but only the barest spark remained. Not even enough to charge an AA battery. She needed to rest to recharge. Dark clouds rumbled above her. Recharge…

Fi turned her face to the sky and the storm.

"Fiona? We need to go."

Fi met Tamsyn's gaze. The woman took a step back. "Yes, you need to go. Now."

The woman took her dad's hand and backed away from the witch. "Your eyes…"

Fi's eyes glowed with the blue-white spark of electricity. "Go. Now."

Voices sounded through the portal. She had to act now. Fi held her palms up high above her head and loosed the last of her electrical magic at the sky. She sent up a prayer to any god or goddess who might hear her. She had one shot at this.

The storm responded to the electrical charge. Lightning flowed down the path her electricity had made, taking the easiest route to earth, through Fi. The last time she had channelled lightning, it had sapped all her strength – and her hair colour, leaving it a bleached white. But she had more control over her magic now, and she knew what she was doing. She hoped.

She stood in the lightning bolt, eyes closed against the brightness of pure natural electricity. Her skin tingled and her hair flew out in a static halo around her head.

Every part of her body felt alive as the lightning caressed her skin with a buzzing sensation. She laughed. Why didn't she ride storms like this more often? Fi felt that she could fly, that she could do anything as she absorbed the electrical power, feeding her magic.

The voices through the portal came louder now. This was her chance. She lowered her hands, pointing them at the circular standing stone. Electricity arced from her palms as she channelled the lightning at the rock. The hole in the centre shimmered violet as her magic hit the fae portal.

A sticky sensation touched on her back teeth as the fae magic fought back. More power. She needed more power.

Fi raised one hand above her head and called down more lightning. The sky responded, keen to release its electrical charge. Her world narrowed to the sensation of magic as the bolts came thick and fast, hitting her with their power. So much electricity. Burning hair filled her nostrils. Her own hair. She couldn't keep this up.

With a scream, Fi launched all of her power at the portal stone. A crack reverberated across the moor and the fae magic flickered then vanished.

Fi sank to her knees. She sucked in a breath, weak and exhausted after absorbing and expending so much magic so quickly. At least she hadn't passed out. The earthy smell of rain combined with the sharp scent of scorched rock. She looked at the grey standing stones, their wet surface shining in a sudden shaft of sunlight.

The circular one had a large crack halfway up the right-hand side. Either side of the split, black rock glinted in the remaining daylight. She crawled forward and held up a hand to touch the burned stone. It was smooth and hot to touch, unlike the roughness of the rest of the rock. Fi squinted. Was it glass?

She used the stone to pull herself upright, wobbling and wincing as all her joints felt like they were on fire. Fi leant against the rock, breathing hard. She had done it. The rain was a soft, cold sensation over her exposed skin. She closed her eyes.

Her hands shook as she pulled out her phone to call it in and swore. Her mobile had melted in the heat. She shivered and looked down. Her clothes fell from her in strips of burned material. She swore again. Only the shredded scraps of her jeans remained.

"Fiona!" Tamsyn called as she sprinted over to Fi, her eyes wide. "Here, take my jacket. You nearly gave Da a heart attack."

Fi pulled on the jacket, flinching as it scraped her raw skin. She leaned on the landlady and accepted her support as they wound their way back down to the road, the path free from Joan's illusions now she was cut off from the human realm.

Back at the tent, the detective stared at Fi. "What the hell was that?"

She sounded so much like Agent Jones that Fi felt a giggle rushing up inside her. "Not hell, just the fae realm. I'll write it up in a report," Fi burst into laughter at the absurdity of it. She had just fought for her life, escaped a horde of piskies, lost Demelza and destroyed a portal. And now she had to write a report. It was crazy.

"Does she need medical attention?" the detective directed her question to Tamsyn with a frown.

"I think she just needs to get home. We'll take her." Tamsyn headed for the van, her arm tight around Fi's waist.

Chapter 39

"You shouldn't have gone without me."

"You were injured…"

"And you're lucky you don't have third degree burns. Tamsyn told me what you did." Mort's voice softened as he peeled what remained of her clothes from her skin. "Drink some more of this." Mort handed her a potion he had gotten from his well-stocked first aid kit. She took a swig and her head went fuzzy. It tasted of caramel and spice, much more palatable than the *Cure All* he had forced her to drink as soon as she'd stepped through the door of the holiday cottage.

"What was the piskie queen like?"

Fi grimaced. "Nasty. She was sort of fat and bigger than other piskies and she was mean. Oh, and she had this giant pet toad that she made me fight. Hey," Fi twisted on the sofa, "did you know that the X-men got it wrong. Toads don't explode when you hit them with lightning."

"O…K…"

I knew I should have gone with you.

"You had to watch, Mort." She took another drink.

"Not too much, that's a strong painkiller."

I did watch him. I listened to him snore for the whole afternoon, then I had to listen to him rant when he woke up and realised you'd gone.

"You were worried about me?" Fi flicked her eyes to the doctor, struggling to focus on his face. That potion was strong stuff.

"Of course I was bloody worried about you! I don't know why you're always so surprised that I care."

Fi gazed up at Mort, her head light and she gave him a dopey smile. "It's sweet." She sighed and closed her eyes. "I worry about you too…I think I love you."

You do?

Fi's eyes snapped open. What had she said?

Mort's face morphed from frustrated to a loopy grin and he knelt beside her. "You do?"

"Do what?"

"Love me."

"Did I say that?"

"Yep."

Definitely. Fi could feel the smugness coming off of the wyrm in waves through her familiar bond.

Fi blushed. What could she say now? Stupid painkillers, making her feel things and worse, tell them to everyone. But it was out in the open now. She'd spent so long worrying about this relationship, about how she would mess it up and the one thing she hadn't seen coming was that she'd fallen in love with Mort and now she'd messed it up in a way she never thought possible; by being too expressive with her feelings.

Mort brushed his lips against hers. "It's OK. I love you, too."

Fi sank into his kiss. Maybe the painkillers weren't so bad after all.

"You know," Mort said as he pulled back, "we still have one more day here in Cornwall…how about we unpack one of the consoles you brought and have a lazy day playing video games tomorrow? Unless you want to talk about what happened, it sounds traumatic and I'd be happy to listen."

Fi reviewed her encounter with the queen and the death match with the toad. She shook her head. Maybe she'd talk about it in detail in time, but for now she wanted to write up the darned report and put it out of her head and decompression time spent actually enjoying her holiday with her boyfriend sounded amazing.

"Sounds perfect," Fi matched Mort's grin, "but I think we could fit in a walk along a beach as well."

Maybe they could salvage the last twenty-four hours of their couples' holiday.

Chapter 40

"Pull over!"

Mort slammed on the brakes and pulled into a layby. "What's wrong?"

"Be back in a minute."

Fi jumped out of the car and ran into the small shop. She returned three minutes later carrying a brown paper bag.

"What's that?"

"Fudge. Mum wanted some."

"Bloody hell, Fi, I thought something was wrong!"

"There would be if I forgot to bring something back for Mum. And Aggy. Hang on a minute."

Fi raced back into the shop and came back out, arms laden with bags of fudge.

"Who's all that for?"

"I panicked. This is for Aggy. And I got some for Bea. And some road fudge."

"What's road fudge?"

"Fudge for us to eat on the way back."

"Don't we already have the pasties from our landlady?"

"Yeah, but…road fudge." Fi shook the bag at him.

Mort shook his head, but he had a smile on his lips. "Who am I to argue with road fudge?"

Fi grinned and did up her seat belt, glad she didn't have to drive back. She cleared her throat.

"Look, I'm sorry our holiday was…just sorry."

"I knew time away with you would be different. But, I'll admit I didn't expect killer piskies and to have the fate of an entire race on our hands."

Fi hugged herself. She had another death on her shoulders – two more if you counted Demelza, which she did – and her dreams now contained a giant toad hunting her down. She blinked and refocused on the conversation. "Agent Jones sorted it all out."

"How?"

"I guess she banged some heads together after I debriefed her, but piskies are still a protected magical species." Knowing her boss, there may well have been some literal banging of heads together.

"And the attacks have stopped?"

Fi nodded. "Now the portal to the fae realm has been shut off, the stones have lost their power. Agent Jones has co-opted Tamsyn and Austol into visiting all the tourist sites to double check, but it looks like the piskies are back to their wild selves stealing chips."

"The portal can't be reopened, can it?"

Fi put a hand on Mort's knee to reassure him. "Not that one. The Magical Liaison Office are working with the government to turn it into a protected site and Agent Jones has reported Joan to some sort of fae representative. From what Maxi said, the fae wasn't happy." Fi hadn't been there for that meeting, but Maxi had texted her updates.

"A job well done, then."

"Yup."

Don't sound too happy about it.

"You don't seem pleased…" Mort echoed Cressida's words.

"You're not my therapist."

"No, I'm your boyfriend who loves you, remember."

Fi gave him a half smile. "Sorry, it's just…my stupid power. It destroys everything. Even when I try to do things right, I still end up blowing someone up."

Mort stopped the car again and reached over to cup her face in his hands. "Listen to me carefully. Everything you did, you did for the right reasons. And your power is exceptional. Just like you. Do you understand me?"

Fi nodded. He leaned in and kissed her. The car behind them honked its horn as it passed and they pulled apart in time to see the driver shooting them an unfriendly hand gesture for good measure.

Cressida cleared her throat. *I have decided.*

"Decided what?" asked Fi, pulling away from Mort and swivelling in her seat to look at her familiar.

You may create me a social media account.

Fi stared at the wyrm.

I cannot deprive the world of my wisdom and the public clearly crave me, so you may create me an account where I can share my advice.

Fi blinked. What had she unleashed on the world?

Whenever you're ready. No rush.

Shaking her head, Fi turned back to Mort and filled him in. "She wants a social media account."

Any time you like.

"I'll open you an account when we get home, OK? We'd better get going if we want to be back by nightfall."

Mort gazed into her blue eyes for a long second before he nodded. He drove for a full minute in silence before he spoke. "Pass me a piece of road fudge."

Fi grinned and handed him a chunk of triple chocolate before stuffing a piece into her own mouth. He always knew the right thing to say.

Epilogue

Fi clenched the steering wheel and stole a glance at the examiner who sat next to her. The woman's head bobbed as she tallied up the marks on the clipboard.

Fi grimaced. She hadn't made that many mistakes, had she?

"Well, Miss Blair, I'm pleased to confirm that with nine minors, you have passed your driving test. Well done."

"Really?"

"Really." The woman handed over the piece of paper and Fi stared at it. There it was, in black and white. She had finally done it. Her heart felt like it could float from her chest.

"Thank you."

The examiner gave a small smile as she exited the car and Fi continued to stare at the paper.

"Well?" Agatha's face appeared by the window. "I saw the examiner come in…how did it go?"

Fi held up the paper. "I passed!"

Her sister's face broke into a wide grin. "Congratulations! Do you want to drive home?"

Fi thought for a moment. Her first road trip as a qualified driver… "Yes."

Agatha climbed in the passenger side and nodded to her sister before pulling out her phone. Fi checked the mirrors again and pulled out, almost colliding with a learner starting their test.

"On second thoughts, maybe you should drive back."

"No, you've got this." Agatha's face was pale and she couldn't quite hide the tremor in her voice as she replied.

"OK, sure." Fi took a breath. "Check mirrors…look both ways…and pull out," Fi muttered. She continued to talk to herself the entire way back to her mother's house, ignoring the way Agatha gripped her seat any time they got too close to the car in front and resisting any urges to swear at the drivers who beeped her for taking her time at a junction until she pulled up into the drive outside her mother's Bed & Breakfast. Why had she thought that driving would equal freedom and independence? Her nerves jangled and her power curled close to the surface, waiting for a blip in her emotional control to leap free and shock something.

"Well done, Fi," Agatha said again, jumping out of the car.

Fi tried to ignore the slight shake in her sister's walk. The drive home hadn't been that bad. She followed Agatha to the back door where the house flung the stable door open wide to let them in. Strange. The semi-sentient house was never normally that welcoming.

She stepped into the kitchen and a bomb exploded. Her power flooded through her on instinct, and she raised her hands, electricity crackling over her fingers.

Calm down, it's a party.

Fi blinked at her familiar's words and took in the scene in the kitchen. A congratulations banner spanned the wall and underneath it, her mother, Mort, Agatha and Liv grinned as smoke wafted from spent party poppers.

"What's all this?"

"We wanted to say congratulations, on passing your test," Liv said, placing her popper on the table.

"If you could lose the magic, Fiona, we can get started." Her mother banged her cane on the ground for emphasis and Agatha jumped to one side to avoid the metal tip as it hit the floor. Agatha rolled her eyes. Their mother had become a menace with the stick in the short time that she'd had it; no one's feet were safe.

"Yes, right." Fi forced her power back down at her mother's request.

Cressida wound around her feet, her scales glinting in the warm light of the kitchen. Almost all of the burnished scales had moulted and her scale rot was gone.

Mort stepped forward and whispered, "Congratulations," in her ear, his hot breath sending a warm trickle through her as he moved to plant a kiss on her lips.

"Thanks everyone, but, how did you know I'd pass?"

"Agatha texted us on the drive back." Fi glanced at her sister who waved her phone like she'd completed a complex undercover mission. "And this came for you." Her mum handed over a post card with a panda holding a sign that read 'You did it'.

Fi turned it over, a smile curving her lips as she caught the name 'Effie' at the bottom.

Congratulations on passing your driving test, I knew you would. And remember to choose an electric car when you buy one next month. All my love, Effie. PS Your gift will cause trouble, think twice.

That was the problem with having a psychic as a friend, they knew everything, but what was the part about a gift?

"Er, Effie said something about a gift?"

"Fiona! Don't be so ungrateful, there's a cake!"

Mort coughed. "I got you a little something…" he handed over a box wrapped in shiny paper. Fi smiled at him and took it, her stomach plummeting. What had he got her that could cause trouble? He looked at her expectantly. She unwrapped it slowly, taking her time. He thought she'd like it…what if she had to destroy it…and then it was open.

"I hope you like it."

She grinned at him and held up the small videogame kart so that the others could see. Nothing dangerous in a plastic keyring. "I love it."

"Just don't drive like in those games."

"Fat chance," Agatha snorted.

Fi gave her sister a look. Her birthday was coming up and Fi was on the hunt for an appropriately bad present after the last two years of gifts from her 'niece'. Fi knew that Agatha was behind the hideous ladybird umbrella and the chicken leg socks…she just needed to find a gnome that was ugly enough to hit Agatha where it hurt; in her garden.

"Come on Fi, cut the cake."

Fi took the proffered knife and smiled. Gnomes were a problem for another day, her sister's birthday was still a couple of months away.

She cut generous portions of the gooey chocolate cake and placed them onto the matching plates her mother had stacked on the table. For now, she had cake and a driving licence. Life was good.

Thank you

A special thank you to my amazing patrons: Emma Ward and Mark Canty who always support me.

If you want to support Gemma, you can find her on www.patreon.com/G_Clatworthy for exclusive first reads of new stories.

Learn more about the magic roundabout and what is sealed under the tricky multiple roundabout system with my short story Summer Solstice in Swindon.

You can also join her newsletter at www.gemmaclatworthy.com for a free prequel to her Rise of Dragons series and follow Gemma on www.instagram.com/gemmaclatworthy, www.facebook.com/gemmaclatworthy or join the Facebook reader's group Gemma's book wyrms.

You can also join her newsletter for a free prequel to her Rise of Dragons series and follow Gemma on www.instagram.com/gemmaclatworthy, www.facebook.com/gemmaclatworthy or join the readers' group Gemma's book wyrms.

About the Author

Gemma started writing during the 2020 lockdown and loves fantasy fiction and dragons in particular. She lives in Wiltshire with her family and two cats and also enjoys crafts of all kinds. You can see all her writing on www.patreon.com/G_Clatworthy. Join the conversation at Gemma's book wyrms readers' group on Facebook.

She also writes children's books. You can find out more on her website www.gemmaclatworthy.com or follow her on Instagram (www.instagram.com/gemmaclatworthy) or Facebook (www.facebook.com/gemmaclatworthy).

Other Books by G Clatworthy

Books in the Rise of the Dragons series:

Awakening

Solstice of Dragons

Equinox Betrayal

Darkest Deception

Attack on Avalon

Fated Bloodlines

Books in the Omensford series (set in the Rise of the Dragons universe):

Bedsocks and Broomsticks

Cream Teas and Crystal Balls

Donkeys and Demons

Pumpkins and Popstars

Exes and Enchantments

Fae and Familiars

Gnomes and Necromancy

Children's Books

The Child Who series:

The Girl Who Lost Her Listening Ears

The Boy Who Lost His Listening Ears

The Girl Who Dreamed of Sleep

The Boy Who Dreamed of Sleep

Nanny Pastry series:

Nanny Pastry and the Nimble Ninjabread Man

Other books:

Coronavirus in the words of children

www.ingramcontent.com/pod-product-compliance
Lightning Source LLC
Chambersburg PA
CBHW031236210726

48287CB00003B/793